Ashl

~

Dodgeball Mystery

Ashleigh M. Garrison ♡

Detroit, Michigan

August 16, 2014

Dodgeball Mystery is a work of fiction. The names, characters, places and incidents are the product of the author's imagination and are not true to life. Any likeness of events and persons, dead or alive are coincidental.

Published by Spread Your Wings Publishing LLC
P.O. Box 760454
Lathrup Village, MI 48076

Cover Design by Hubert Massey, PhD

Printed in the United States of America
ISBN –13: 978-0-9792080-3-4
ISBN–10: 0-9792080-3-3

This novel is dedicated to my late grandfather, Aubrey C. Garrison, my grandmother, Hope Garrison, and all of the young readers out there; never stop reading.

Acknowledgments

I would like to first thank God; for without him, none of this would be possible.

Thank you to my parents, Donnell and Kelly Garrison. I am forever indebted to you, and forever grateful for the life you have provided me.

Thank you to the rest of my family as well (I cannot name all of you); you are all so supportive, and I really do appreciate you.

I would also like to recognize my family at Church of the New Covenant-Baptist, which has always loved me and encouraged me.

I would like to say thank you to Marquita L. Scott and the rest of the Spread Your Wings Publishing Company for helping me and guiding me.

Also, thank you to Mr. Hubert Massey, the incredibly talented artist who designed my book cover.

To my best friends (Elyse and Rumer), thank you for always being incredibly supportive. I appreciate and love you both so much.

Thank you to Mrs. Smith, my 8th grade science teacher and advisor, who gave me tough love when I needed it the most and pushed me. I will never forget the things you did for me, as well as those amazing science videos.

Chapter 1
The Announcement

Kristin Gregory was sixteen years young and proud to say so ever since April 13th. Her hair was the perfect length; it went past her shoulders, but not all the way down to her back. She had tried incredibly hard the summer of eighth grade to grow it out, so that she would fit in with the popular girls at school. In eighth grade, she and her best friend Elizabeth were the only girls with shoulder length hair; apparently, it was officially uncool not to have long hair. Kristin had always loved her hair. Not just its light, honey brown color, but the texture as well. It was thick, but not too thick. She could do a lot with it, but she usually chose to wear it straight. She'd always gotten compliments on her hair; it was naturally beautiful, smooth, and with lighter tips–kind of a dirty blonde. People always asked her if she had her hair dip-dyed and her answer was always the same–No. Part of the love she had for her hair came from the fact that everyone else loved it, but mostly, she was in love with her hair because that was just her opinion.

Her eyes were a different story. Although she did not think they were ugly, she didn't think they were beautiful either. She thought they were pretty plain. They were an average brown color, but in the summer they became a tad lighter. Kristin had to admit that she thought she was a good-looking person. Not gorgeous but good-looking. A solid seven and a half out of ten.

When Kristin was in fourth grade, her father passed away. His death was a sudden one, and between Kristin and her mother, Kristin had definitely taken the death the hardest. Immediately following his death, Kristin found it easiest to move on with life like nothing had happened at all. When her mother first broke the news that he had been killed in combat, Kristin broke down into tears. She sobbed for an entire day. She couldn't eat or even think straight. The next day she woke up and decided to push her father's death to the back of her mind. Kristin tried to pretend that everything was fine. She continued with her daily routines. All of her teachers were concerned and contacted Mrs. Gregory, because they felt that her calm disposition was just not normal after such a tragic loss. With all that was happening around her, it was easy for Kristin to push his death aside. After he passed, so many things changed. Her world was turned upside down.

A month after her father's funeral, her mother got a great job at a music studio. This new job couldn't have come at a better time; when Kristin's father died, they were left with a pile of bills and debt to pay off and Kristin's mother didn't even have a job. In fact, they were about to lose their house. That's when Kristin's mother landed the job at JR Music Studio, a local music studio in Michigan, where she was responsible for bringing in new talent every month. Mrs. Showers, the mother of Kristin's best friend Elizabeth, had recommended Kristin's mother for the job and had pretty much gotten it for her. Mrs. Gregory had loved the job instantly.

After about a month of having this new job, and not to mention the huge income it was bringing, Kristin knew her life would never be the same. Kristin and her mother had moved into a big, new house. Both of their wardrobes had widened and became lavish, and Kristin had transferred from her public school to Eldridge Preparatory Academy. Eldridge was the most prestigious school in the state, partly because of the low acceptance rate and academics, and partly because of the expensive tuition. Getting her mother to allow her to change schools had not been easy. However, once Kristin showed her the test scores, Mrs. Gregory began to consider it. The fact that the school went up to twelfth grade was just icing on the cake. When she moved to Elizabeth's school, Kristin realized that her average jeans, crop tops, and Converse sneakers just would not do at her new school. All of the popular girls were dressed head to toe in designer clothes, so Kristin threw out her entire wardrobe and got a completely new one. Instead of focusing on grieving and her father's death, Kristin threw herself into creating a totally new appearance. The new Kristin always looked polished when she left her house. She always made sure that her makeup was just right, her outfit was cute, and her hair was well styled.

Unlike Kristin, Elizabeth did not buy expensive clothes like the popular girls at Kristin's school. Her clothes were cute, but they weren't expensive. She shopped at stores like Target and Forever 21. Elizabeth always said that she would rather spend her money on things more important. She liked cute clothes, but she wasn't a fan of shopping for hours and spending hundreds of dollars. Whereas Kristin absolutely hated school, except the parts of it when she could chat with her friends, Elizabeth loved school and learning. Education was an important aspect of her life. Kristin loved pop music and was always listening to the latest songs, and Elizabeth usually could not stand the annoying songs by boy bands that all the girls at school bellowed out in the school hallways. Kristin adored shopping, but Elizabeth preferred reading a good book or watching a movie. Everything that Kristin did had to be huge and out-there and Elizabeth just preferred to keep to herself and to not draw attention. Elizabeth lived with both of her parents and had never seen any financial struggles in her life and Kristin's father was deceased and she had never really been rich until her mother got the job at JR. Pretty much the only thing they had in common was their love of good Italian food, but somehow they got along great.

Elizabeth and Kristin met when they were both ten years old while at a park in Birmingham, a comfortable and picture-perfect suburb in southeast Michigan. Both girls lived in Birmingham; however, Elizabeth lived in a huge mansion, while

Kristin resided in a small home. They were ten years old when they came across each other at the swings. When Kristin transferred to Elizabeth's school in fourth grade, both girls were ecstatic. In sixth grade, Kristin befriended Eliza Parker and introduced Eliza to Elizabeth. "It's like you guys are meant to be friends. Your names sound so similar. Guys, I'm sure this is destiny," Kristin had told Eliza and Elizabeth when she introduced them.

Ever since Eliza and Elizabeth's meeting, the three of them would hang out. They soon became a little trio. The girls did everything together. Everyone in school knew that they were best friends. Most would even describe them as inseparable. Every Thursday since they had met, Elizabeth came over to Kristin's house and the girls ate dinner together. When Eliza came into the picture, the two girls added her to the tradition. Kristin had never been so close with anyone (besides family, of course) the way she was close with Elizabeth and Eliza. The friendship between them was just easy. They all shared secrets with each other. Sadly, Eliza had cut all ties with Elizabeth and Kristin. The girls had had a falling out. Now, Eliza was the enemy. Just looking at her made Kristin sick to her stomach, which was why she tried to avoid her as best as she could at school. Today was Thursday. Elizabeth would be over soon. Kristin was beginning to get antsy while waiting. She hated being alone in that big house. As she tapped her foot impatiently, she wondered where her mother could be.

Kristin sat in her living room of her beautiful,

yet cozy mansion. Kristin's house sat in a wooded, gated community. Everything about it screamed prestige and wealth. Expensive cars were lined up in every house's driveway. Her neighbors included doctors, lawyers, and famous professional athletes. A few big time actors had even settled in the suburban neighborhood. Their wives wore Gucci and Burberry outfits and spent most of their days shopping or lounging. Most of them didn't clean their houses or tend to their own children; they had housekeepers and nannies for that. The mansions resembled the ones that were featured on MTV's Cribs. Sometimes it all still amazed Kristin. She never could have imagined that she would live in such a gorgeous place. Her house was almost all the way in the back of the community, so you practically had to drive through the entire subdivision to reach her house. After about ten minutes of driving down a curved path, a colonial, brick mansion could be spotted. It was easy for Kristin to describe her house to people who were trying to find it; she always told them it was the only house with a brick water fountain in front of it. On both sides of the fountain were angels made of stone. The angels had been Mrs. Gregory's idea. She had claimed that they symbolized the protection that God put around their family. The angels held American flags in their hands, which were put there in memory of Mr. Gregory.

Every time that Kristin passed them, she smiled a little. At first, she would almost cringe. Kristin had come to realize that the old saying, "Time heals all wounds" was far from true. However, it did make things a lot easier. Now, she could look at something that made her think about him and not feel like she was going to break. She could look at a picture of him and not want to curl up into a ball. She could even talk about him and laugh at all the funny times they shared together. Although he had been in the army since Kristin was six, she used to see him for most of the holidays. He truly was a kindhearted man, especially towards his only daughter.

Directly behind the fountain, you could usually find Mrs. Gregory's black Mercedes car parked in the circular driveway. Directly behind it was Kristin's car. The front door to Kristin's house was your ordinary, wooden door, except for the fact that there was a prestigious looking "G" engraved on the door. From the outside, her house was traditional and classic, and on the inside, it was no different, except for a few discrepancies. The first thing that most people noticed when walking through the front door was the amazing staircase that was a few feet away from it. It was a spiral staircase made of white marble. In fact, much of Kristin's house was comprised of beautiful marble. Originally, the house was mostly carpeted. Mrs. Gregory changed this two days after occupying the house. Kristin's living room was grand and fancy. There were a few pictures of Kristin, her parents, her grandparents, and other estranged relatives, which lined the walls. Kristin's favorite photo was one of her mother, father, and herself. It had been taken at her fourth birthday party. Her face was painted, her father was wearing cat ears, and her mother was making a silly face. That photograph summed up the dynamic of Kristin's family before her father's death. Everyone was always laughing and having a good time. They could joke around with each other. The picture reminded Kristin of the good times. Comfortable couches and chairs filled the room. An actual Picasso painting hung on the back wall of the living room, being that Mrs. Gregory adored art. Right next to it was a seventy-five-inch LED TV, which was easily one of Kristin's favorite things in the house. On the other side of the TV was a painting of Kristin's from kindergarten.

Kristin sat on the couch and checked her gold Cartier watch—a sixteenth birthday present from her mother. It was 5:30 p.m. Where was her mother? Probably working overtime, or chatting with co-workers. Or, she could be stuck in traffic. Michigan's traffic didn't compare to New York or anything, but rush hour could get pretty crazy. Kristin sat watching old cartoons; she was pretty bored and did not have any homework. She then picked up her phone and started having a text conversation with one of her friends to try and get rid of her boredom. Just then, her mother walked in the door. Kristin could hear her mother's expensive Jimmy Choo heels clicking on the fine expensive granite floors. She heard them getting closer. Her mother approached the living room.

"Hey, darling," she said kindly.

Kristin took in her mother's beauty. She one hundred percent believed that her mother was the most beautiful person on the planet. Her chestnut brown hair fell to her shoulders and her figure resembled that of a supermodel. Out of all things, Kristin most envied her mother's beautiful eyes.

They were light brown eyes with faint specks of pretty green in them. Kristin's mother always looked amazing; almost like she had just stepped out of the spa and into a new designer outfit. That was just how Mrs. Gregory was, always so put-together. But, just like Kristin, she had a more relaxed side, in which she would lounge wearing sweatpants with her hair tied up. As much as Mrs. Gregory and Kristin both hated to admit it, designer apparel and the lavish life just weren't who they really were. At heart, they were just simple people who were fortunate to experience the finer things in life.

"Hi." She did not seem to be her usual self. She never once looked up from her phone. A cloud of gloom could easily be felt above her. Had she only known what was going to happen in the future, maybe she would've been more appreciative of that day.

"How was school?" Her mother kicked off her shoes and propped her feet up on the coffee table.

Kristin looked at her mother's manicured feet. Doing so made Kristin realize that she herself needed a trip to the nail salon. That place always managed to calm her down. It was her "happy place" as they call it. She loudly exhaled. "I can't even begin to tell you. School was terrible," Kristin said. Feeling the weight on her shoulders slowly lift, she looked down at her watch and touched the smooth diamonds on it, thinking about her horrible experiences at school.

Her mother put her arm around Kristin's shoulder and asked, "Why was it so terrible?"

Kristin whined, "Well, all of my teachers were either sick or out of town. Apparently, some flu is going around. The school couldn't get enough substitutes for the day, so the entire ninth grade had to go to classrooms of another grade. But, they didn't send me to just any grade. I got sent to a first grade classroom! Principal Edwards said that it would be a good chance to bond with "younger generations." Isn't that so stupid?" She flipped her long hair over her shoulder.

"I was going to say that it's interesting but I guess it's a matter of opinion," her mother replied. She gave Kristin's shoulders a tight squeeze. "I'm sorry you had such a bad day but hey, look at it this way: At least your teachers weren't there to give you any homework, right?" Her mother raised an eyebrow, as if saying: *Am I right or am I right?*

Kristin said, "I'd rather have five hours of homework than go through what I went through today. Gosh, I'm so grateful that you didn't have any other children." For a split second, she closed her eyes and imagined their house filled with the sound of toddlers running rampant. She shivered at the mere thought and ripped her eyes open. After a few moments of silence, Kristin commented, "I'm starving."

"I'm going to start making the casserole in a few minutes. Lizzie's coming over tonight, right?"

"Yeah," Kristin said. Thinking about being reunited with her best friend made her cheer up a little.

Her mother replied, "Oh! I almost forgot. I have an announcement. Maybe it will cheer you up."

"Great," Kristin said sarcastically.

"Okay, well I'll take a stab at it anyway. Are you ready for a story that is going to change life as you know it?"

Kristin nodded and cracked a smile at her mother's excessively dramatic voice.

"So today, as I'm in the studio, one of your favorite celebrities walks in. It was Lianna Gibson!" Her mother exclaimed, causing Kristin to scream.

"Oh my Gosh! Oh my Gosh! Oh my Gosh!" she yelled.

Her mother looked pleased.

Kristin was now standing jumping up and down. When she gathered herself she asked, "Are you serious? Do not let this be a joke."

Her mother shook her head no, showing her excited daughter that what she had just said was not a joke.

"Mom, what did you say? Please, don't tell me you said anything embarrassing," Kristin begged.

Mrs. Gregory replied, "No, actually we were having a good conversation. She's having a sixteenth birthday party, and she happened to be at DTE Energy Theater for a concert and an autograph signing, so she came to the studio to catch up with some of the guys in the studio who used to record her demos when she lived here and was up and coming. She was saying how fun it'll be with the great food, celebrities, and entertainment. I started telling her how much you loved her, and she told me you could come to the party."

"Mom, you are the best! I cannot believe this. I'm going to a celebrity's birthday party. And the celebrity is Lianna Gibson. I would cry, but it might ruin the moment."

"You're welcome. The party is Saturday," her mother announced.

"I already know when the party is. Lianna has been tweeting about it for the past week. I have to find shoes, an outfit, decide how to do my hair. Today is Thursday, how on Earth will I do this? Anyway, it doesn't matter, because soon I am officially going to be considered popular." She bragged. Kristin started dancing. She imagined herself hanging out with Lianna, becoming besties. Then Kristin remembered Liz, who was great, but Lianna was a celebrity. An actual celebrity, with fans, fame, and a glam team!

Snapping Kristin out of her thoughts, her mother said, "Wait, there's more. You have to call Lianna today to R.S.V.P. She gave me her number. She figured you'd be excited to talk to her. She's expecting your call; I told her all about you."

"Oh my gosh! I get to talk to her? Where is her number? Where is it?   Where is it?" Kristin demanded. She began squealing.

Kristin's mother dug through her Tory Burch tote bag to find the business card that Lianna had written her number on. When she found it, she handed it to Kristin, whose hands were shaking. She quickly dialed the number into her cell. After three rings, there was an answer.

"Hello?" the perky voice asked.

Kristin could have peed her pants. Here she was hearing the actual voice of her biggest inspiration. "Hi, Lianna. I'm Kristin Gregory and I'm calling to R.S.V.P.," Kristin stated confidently. On the inside, she was dying from excitement.

"Oh, you're Charlotte Gregory's daughter, right?" Lianna asked.

"Y-yeah," Kristin stammered.

"Don't be nervous. I hear you're a fan. I'm so happy you called. I want you to come to my party. I've already added you to the guest list. And you can bring a friend too. I'd tell you that you could bring more than one, but I'm already down to the wire, as far as the guest list goes. "

"No, that's okay. I'm happy that I can even come. Thank you so much, Lianna."

"No problem. Your mom is amazing, so of course I had to repay her for everything. Plus, I always look out for fans. I've been working tirelessly to make this thing great. You have no idea. From food tastings to dress fittings. Gosh, I feel like I've planned a wedding. Only difference is that I'm not marrying a hot guy. I'm exhausted, to be honest," she breathed.

Kristin could not believe that Lianna Gibson was venting to her. She was venting, right? She was sharing her thoughts with a complete stranger. Kristin got such a genuine vibe off of her. They talked for a few more minutes about everyday things. Kristin was shocked that Lianna even had normal person problems. She had always figured that celebrities had people to take care of everything for them.

After she had gotten off the phone with Lianna, her gloomy mood had completely disappeared. Kristin was still in a state of shock when her mother walked back into the living room a few minutes later. She was amazed at how kind Lianna had been. Lianna didn't seem stuck-up or anything close to it. She seemed real. Kristin had just talked to her idol via phone and scored invites to her party. Her life was pretty good right about then. Now that she'd raved, all she needed to do was find something to wear. Life was looking up already. She sat on the couch waiting for Lizzie and watching TV with a small smile on her face. The time passed by quickly, as it always did when she was watching the Kardashians. She was hanging on the edge of the couch, as she watched Khloé and Kim get into an argument. Just as the scene was about to get even better, the doorbell rang. Kristin jumped off the couch excitedly and ran to the door.

"Lizzie!" she exclaimed. "You're finally here!" Elizabeth was naturally radiant. She needed not an ounce of makeup, since her skin was flawless and always seemed to have a glow. Her shoulder-length, dirty blonde hair was pulled back into a bun. That girl could be in rags and still manage to make it look perfect. Kristin, on the other hand, always felt like she had to dress up in public. She just didn't feel as beautiful without a great outfit.

"Wasn't today the craziest day in school ever?" asked Elizabeth.

They were both sitting on the couch with their feet propped up on the coffee table. They began talking about the day and all the events. The simple conversations that the two girls shared was what Kristin appreciated most. They didn't have to be going someplace interesting all the time. They could simply talk. Elizabeth was the person who she trusted most. There was never a dull word said; both girls loved talking, although Kristin loved it more. Elizabeth had always been the better listener. Whenever Kristin had a problem, she would listen to her ramble on and on about it. Once Kristin was finally finished rambling, Elizabeth would offer kind words of advice. Elizabeth had always been good at giving advice. It was her specialty. Along with being Kristin's best friend, she was also her personal therapist.

During the conversation, Kristin said, "I'm super excited about Saturday. You can't even guess how amazing it's going to be." She cupped her hands around her face, dreaming of the wonderful weekend that she thought was ahead of her.

Elizabeth looked confused and replied, "Of course I can. It's my party. You're talking about my birthday party on Friday, right? I'm so happy you'll be there. I was so disappointed when you couldn't come last year. Good thing you're coming this time." Elizabeth caught her breath and continued, "It's going to be awesome. I have everything all planned out. I'm so anxious about it, though."

"Wait–your party is Saturday, as in this Saturday? Three days from today—that Saturday?" Kristin asked.

Elizabeth nodded and then said, "Don't act like you don't remember. I've been blabbing about this party for a whole month, remember?"

Kristin nodded, but on the inside, she was cringing.

She then remembered that Elizabeth's party was that coming Saturday. How could she have forgotten so easily? The party was going to be at Elizabeth's beach house, which was a huge mansion. Everyone was supposed to wear a swimsuit so they could go swimming by the beach. Elizabeth was also setting up activities and games on the beach. Her parents had booked a good DJ and everything. There was supposed to be a dance floor set up so that all of the kids could dance. Elizabeth's mother had gotten a wonderful caterer so that there would be the best food and had spent weeks deciding on which foods to serve. The whole grade was invited practically and everyone was talking about the party. It was supposed to be a lot of fun. Kristin was surprised that Elizabeth was even having a big party because usually she just had an intimate gathering with her closest friends. Kristin began to recall all the times when Elizabeth was going on and on about her party and Kristin was daydreaming about kissing Liam Hemsworth. She then regretted her bad habit of tuning people out.

As she sat there, she felt her stomach twist. Her heart instantly sank when she realized how upset Elizabeth would be if she found out that her best friend would not be able to attend her sixteenth birthday party. She couldn't decide if it would be best to come clean about not being able to go right then, or if she should pretend like she could go. Then, maybe she could fake sick the night of Lizzie's party. It was not the best idea, but at least then she would be able to spare Elizabeth's feelings. She hated lying to her best friend. Then again, wasn't there a quote that said something about it being okay to lie every once in awhile? Kristin stared into space, thinking deeply about the choice she had to make quickly.

"I said what are you doing?" Elizabeth yelled.

She was waving her hands in front of Kristin's face. Finally, Kristin blinked and snapped her head in Elizabeth's direction. Elizabeth had been calling her for the past thirty seconds, but Kristin was too busy thinking.

"Huh?" Kristin asked.

"Ugh, sometimes I swear you don't listen to a thing that I say." Elizabeth paused and continued, "It's always me listening to you."

This was very true. Between the two girls, Kristin was definitely the dominant one in the friendship. She usually made all the plans. She decided when they would hang out, where they would hang out, and what they would do when they hung out. That was just the way it had always been. Kristin was decisive and quick. Elizabeth usually did not have a problem with this. She did not mind Kristin making all the plans, and she would go along with most things. However, Kristin knew not to even try to abuse Elizabeth's easy going personality.

Elizabeth responded, "You couldn't have forgotten about my party!"

Kristin could not think of any words to say.

Elizabeth looked confused, and noticed the worry on Kristin's face. "Are you okay? You look kinda nervous," she said. Elizabeth knew Kristin like the back of her hand.

"W-w-what do you mean? Why would you think that I'm nervous? I am definitely not nervous." Kristin said quickly. She fiddled with her fingers. Elizabeth saw that her hands were all sweaty as Kristen rubbed them on her pants to try and get the sweat off.

21

"Well, for starters, your hands are sweating more than my mom in a hot yoga class," Elizabeth told her. She picked up Kristin's hand, which was covered in sweat, to prove her point.

"Oh, my hands always sweat. I have this terrible disease called sweatitis. I must've forgotten to tell you about it. It makes you sweat on your hands, your forehead, pretty much *everywhere*. You don't wanna know where else I'm sweating right now!" Kristin laughed and then bit her lip nervously.

"First of all," Elizabeth started, "Eww! And second of all, there is no such disease called sweatitis. You totally just made that up. And I would know because I'm a pro in medicine. I know a lot about diseases, remember?"

"I did not make it up. It's real, and I've had it since I was six years old. Truth is, I've been hiding the disease from you this entire time because I was ashamed. I get emotional every time I talk about it. Oh god, I feel the tears coming on," she replied dramatically. Kristin put her head in her hands and started to fake cry, hoping that Elizabeth would buy it. Elizabeth moved closer to Kristin and removed her hands from her face, which was dry. Kristin was caught in the shameful act of fake crying. She had to come clean. Hiding it was never going to work in the first place.

Kristin said, "Okay, fine. The truth is, I cannot go to your birthday party."

Elizabeth said with seriousness in her voice to Kristin, "You have to be joking." Elizabeth's face was tight and her jaw was clenched.

Kristin shifted her eyes towards the ground,

unable to look Elizabeth in the eyes. She spent the next few seconds trying to suck up to Elizabeth. It seemed like no amount of compliments was going to get rid of Elizabeth's anger. After all, it was completely justified. Friends were supposed to be there for each other. Lately, it seemed like Kristin was always bailing. Elizabeth had not said anything to Kristin about it yet; she figured it was a temporary thing. Not to mention the fact that she hated conflict. She had finally reached her breaking point.

"Why can't you go to my party?" Elizabeth asked after a moment of silence.

"Because I'm going to someone else's," Kristin mumbled cautiously.

"You're going to someone else's party? Whose party is it? Who are you ditching me for this time?" She rolled her eyes.

"Lianna Gibson. I cannot turn down this opportunity. She is one of my biggest idols. I can't miss it. This will finally prove to Eliza that I'm not a loser who spends my Friday nights with my *mom*. I mean, just imagine how jealous Eliza would be if she found out that I was at Lianna Gibson's party. Everyone at school will think I'm so cool and I will no longer be that loser who hangs out with her mom on her Friday nights."

"Right! And I'm just your best friend who's been there for you through all of the hard times. Did Lianna make you homemade soup when you were sick? Because I don't think she did."

Kristin felt horrible. She tried to be funny by saying, "Well, your soup wasn't really that good, so now we're even."

Elizabeth's straight face didn't budge. Kristin could tell that her joke had been a failed attempt. She saw the muscles in her friend's face tighten. Kristin could feel her heart beat getting faster by the second. Elizabeth always had Kristin's back. She defended her when the mean girls picked on her, she laughed at her usually not funny jokes, she helped her get through her father's tragic death, and pretty much everything else. Kristin understood why Elizabeth was upset about her not being able to attend, but she also felt that her friend should have been more supportive.

Kristin replied, "You're acting like this is my fault. I had no idea my mom was going to come home today and tell me that I would be going to Lianna Gibson's party. Lianna told me I could bring someone with me. You can come too. Wouldn't that be amazing? That would be the most fun way to celebrate your birthday. Imagine celebrating with Lianna Gibson! That would be so cool."

"Wait, wait, wait! You want me to go to her party on *my* birthday? And what about my party?" Elizabeth reacted.

"Couldn't you cancel it?" Kristin asked a little shakily.

Elizabeth roared, "Cancel my party? Have you lost your mind? You want me to cancel *my* party? My mom spent a lot of money on it. How can you, my best friend, not come? You're being so disrespectful right now, Kristin. I honestly cannot believe you." Elizabeth stood up and snatched her bag from the couch. She made her way towards to door, purposely stomping her feet as loudly as she could.

Luckily, the living room was a good distance from the front door, so Kristin had a little time to think of a way to prevent the argument from escalating. After a couple moments, she got up and began walking in Elizabeth's direction. Kristin did her best to catch up with Elizabeth. As she speed-walked, she wondered when Elizabeth had gotten so fast. Perhaps it had something to do with the cycling classes Elizabeth was taking. She repeatedly called after Elizabeth, but Elizabeth continued. Kristin knew the only way to get Elizabeth to stop was to say something that would upset her. She jogged to catch up to Elizabeth. The two girls were almost nose to nose.

Kristin said, "Ya know, you don't have to be such a brat."

"You did not just say that," Elizabeth said. She put her hand on her hip, something she always did when she was annoyed.

"Yeah, I did. I think it is a little petty that you are getting all worked up about a silly party. I mean, really? Trying to storm out of my house like a kid over a party? I thought you were better than that, Lizzie."

"It's about the fact that as best friends, we should be there for each other. And it feels like you are never there for me." Elizabeth turned towards the door.

Kristin ran a hand through her hair. She said, "Elizabeth, you know I love you. We've always been close, so don't make it seem like I'm the bad one here. Calm down. You don't have to leave. We can talk about this over dinner."

"No, there is no talking. You've obviously made your decision, right?" Elizabeth paused and waited for Kristin to respond. When a few moments of silence passed, she yelled, "Ugh! I don't want to spend another second in this house with you."

"Good because I don't want you here. Get out!" Kristin screamed.

Elizabeth's eyes bulged. Never had Kristin ever said something like that to her. Kristin herself was shocked that the words had come out. Instantly, she regretted it. She wanted to quickly apologize, but her pride got in the way of that. Why should she be the one to apologize first? No. That was not going to happen. Besides, the fight was partly Lizzie's fault too, right? Wasn't she equally as wrong for being so dramatic? Elizabeth knew how much she loved Lianna Gibson. Since she was fourteen, she had been Lianna's fan. When she was a child, she would sit in front of the TV every Friday night and watch Lianna's sitcom–*Life With Lianna*.

Elizabeth walked out the door without saying anything to Kristin. Kristin had a fight with herself over whether or not she should go after her friend. When she finally made the decision, she ran to the door to call Elizabeth. She swung the door open. It was too late. Elizabeth's car was already out of sight. Frustrated, Kristin walked back into the house and slammed her front door. Her mother was waiting by the door when she walked back in. She stood with her arms wide open, offering Kristin a hug. Kristin shook her head and brushed past her mother. She walked up to her room and locked herself in there.

Kristin did everything but sleep that night. She spent most of the night tossing, turning, and laying there thinking about the fight. No matter how hard she tried, she just could not fall asleep. She even put on her sleeping mask. Nothing seemed to be working. Kristin figured she deserved the misery for kicking her best friend out of her house. That night, she prayed to God for a miracle. She prayed that somehow Elizabeth would forget all about the mishap and tried her best to get some rest.

Chapter 2
Knocked Out

The next morning, Kristin's mother had to tell her daughter to get up five times. It was at 7:15 a.m., that she was able to drag herself out of bed. When she looked at the clock on her nightstand, her eyes widened. School started at 8:00 a.m. and she lived about fifteen minutes away. Kristin realized, as she did math calculations in her head, that she only had thirty minutes to get ready. She went through her morning routine much quicker than usual. She did not even have time to put on any makeup. Her hair was pulled back into a high ponytail. At first, Kristin had considered running her straightener through it quickly, but she realized she just did not have time. She ran over to her walk-in closet. It was easily triple the size of the average person's room. On the glass, double-doors, the letter "K" was engraved in a large, cursive font.

All of the walls of the closet were white. There were crystal chandeliers and some silver chairs. First walking in, you would see a room that contained all of her shirts, accessories, underclothes, and shoes. Everything was color-coordinated, thanks to the help of Kristin's mother and their housekeeper, Nancy. The shirts and jackets were against the left wall. On the right wall were her shoes, which included Louboutins, Chanel boots, Converse, Vans, Toms, Michael Kors flats and sandals, and much more. To the right of the shoes was a huge dresser that contained her underclothes. Next to it was a much smaller one, which was where she kept most of her jewelry. The really expensive pieces were held in a safe under her bed. Kristin entered her closet and grabbed a fuchsia silk blouse that she spotted. It still had the price tag on it–$300. She also pulled a black blazer. She then walked over to the flats section of her shoes. She spotted her favorite pair of black Tory Burch flats and grabbed them from the top shelf. Kristin ran to the next room of her closet. In that room were her pants and skirts. Kristin had more jeans that anyone could ever imagine. The mall was like a second home to her. She could be spotted there at least once a week, maybe more. Plus, her mother was an online shopping fanatic, so she was constantly buying Kristin new things. Kristin appreciated anything her mother bought her, but jeans were always her first choice. Her jean supply was so large that it was separated into sections by brand. Kristin's five favorite jean brands were J Brand, 7 For All Mankind, Joe's, Paige Denim, and Guess. As far as she was concerned, other brands did not even come close. She pulled down a pair of dark wash Sevens and rushed to change.

After examining herself in the mirror, she knew that she would certainly not win a best-dressed award. Her blouse was tucked into her pants. The blazer helped to tie the outfit together, though Kristin still was not impressed with herself. Kristin walked over to her nightstand and grabbed her pearl necklace. The necklace had been passed down from her father's side of the family. He never got to chance to actually give it to her, because it was always given to the daughter on her sixteenth birthday. Her grandparents had traveled from West Virginia to Michigan to give her the necklace. Every time she put it on, she thought of her father. A picture of the two of them was on her nightstand. She smiled at the picture a little before exiting her room.

"Kristin," her mother called, just as she was making her way into the kitchen. "Oh, hi, darling. You look cute."

Kristin shot her mother a look. She walked over to the counter and picked up an apple. "What?"

"You look beautiful, as always, darling." Her mother gave her a kiss on the head, and Kristin took a bite of her apple.

"I couldn't really fall asleep last night. I think I probably got three hours of sleep."

"Still thinking about the fight with Lizzie?"

Kristin nodded.

"I'm sorry, dear."

"Can you drive me today? I'm too tired," Kristin said.

"I want to, but I've got a meeting in..." Mrs. Gregory paused to look at her watch, "Fifteen minutes. I ordered you a car. It should be out there now, darling. By the way, you left your phone on your nightstand last night. I charged it up for you and put it on the side of your backpack."

"Thanks, Mommy." Kristin grabbed a bottle of water out of the refrigerator and hugged her mother good-bye. She slowly walked to the front door and grabbed her backpack. She took a deep breath as she stepped outside.

There, she saw William waiting for her in front of a town car. William was the driver her mother always requested whenever they needed a car service. Kristin did not use the car service as often as her mother. She much preferred to drive herself places, but it was pretty convenient. The good thing about it was that William always had a nonfat caramel frappuccino waiting for her in the car.

"Morning, William," she said.

"Good morning, Miss Kristin," he replied. He opened the door for her. At 5'8", she had to duck a little to enter the car. She spotted her frappuccino and sighed a sigh of relief.

As they drove further, Kristin began hoping that they would run into some traffic. Kristin gazed out the window. She was nervous to see Elizabeth. Trying to distract herself, she pulled out her phone and checked her social media accounts. *"Nothing new,"* she thought as she scrolled. She then went to Elizabeth's page. It was filled with posts about new books or movies that had come out, as well as pictures of she and her friends. Kristin's eyes widened when she realized Elizabeth had deleted all the pictures of she and Kristin. How could she be so rash? So they had one fight. Big whoop. That was no reason to go deleting pictures. Kristin knew the girls at school would be suspicious. Now, everyone was going to think they were fighting.

The last thing Kristin needed was pathetic, freshman girls (and even some D-list sophomores) coming up to her and asking about her personal life. Wide-eyed, high-pitched fourteen-year-olds were the most annoying creatures on Earth. Yes, Kristin found it to be cute that they looked up to her in a way. She had the best clothes, a luxurious life, and pretty good grades. All her ducks seemed to be in a row. However, she also found them to be bothersome when they would approach her 24/7.

Kristin exhaled loudly as they pulled onto her school's campus. It was practically a mini college, offering a pool, a hockey arena, a spa, and more. The entrance to the school was covered in greenery. Although she was having a tough day, the flowers and trees managed to make her feel the slightest ounce of happiness. There was a huge car line leading up to the gates. The entrance was sort of set up like border crossing. Each car had to go through and speak to the security guard, who sat in the teller booth. There were ten tellers set up. This was not nearly enough. It seemed like forever until Kristin's car finally reached the gate. She showed her student ID to the teller.

"Morning, Miss Gregory. Have a nice day," the man said.

"Thanks, you too," she replied in the least sad tone she could speak in.

Kristin's car pulled up to the upper school, and she gathered her things. She checked her phone. It was only 7:50 a.m. to her surprise. William let Kristin out of the car, and they said good-bye to each other. Kristin walked through the doors of the school. Immediately to the right was the main office and dean's office. When you walked forward and turned left, there were the ninth and tenth grade hallways. In the opposite direction were the eleventh and twelfth grade hall, dining hall, and gym. Straight across from the entrance was the library.

Kristin took a sip of her frappuccino and made her way to her locker. A few girls pointed and whispered when she passed. She was sure they were talking about her appearance. She swallowed hard and tried to block them out. Elizabeth's locker was right next to hers. She kept hoping that Elizabeth would be somewhere else instead. As she turned a corner, she was sure that the universe was against her that day. There stood Elizabeth. She was unloading her backpack. Kristin stopped walking and adjusted her blazer. She crossed her fingers and started walking again. She reached Elizabeth's locker, causing her to look up from her backpack. Elizabeth saw Kristin and rolled her eyes. She went back to unloading her bag. Both girls had gym first hour.

"So you're giving me the silent treatment?" Kristin asked.

Elizabeth reached up to put her Biology book in her locker, but clumsily dropped it.Kristin quickly grabbed it and handed it to her. Elizabeth snatched the book.

"Can I at least get a thank you?"

Elizabeth muttered through her teeth, "Thank you, Kristin."

"I assume you're still mad with me," Kristin said.

"I'm not just mad with you, I'm done with you.

This friendship is over!" Elizabeth announced. "I'm sick of being treated badly."

"Lizzie, that's a little rash, don't ya think?" Kristin chuckled a bit. She flipped her shiny hair over her shoulder.

"No, I don't. And don't call me Lizzie. My name is Elizabeth."

"You wanna know something? You're really being a jerk about this. You're ending our friendship over a party? I cannot believe you. And you wanna know something else?" Kristin's blood was boiling. Initially, she had planned on making things right with her friend. Things had changed drastically since the start of the conversation.

"Not really," Elizabeth told her.

"Well, I'm telling you anyway. I don't want to be friends with someone who's so annoying. So if you're done with me, I'm done with you too." Kristin folded her arms. Past Elizabeth, she spotted Eliza, who was walking towards them. Eliza was looking perfect as ever. Her light blonde hair was bouncy with curls, her heels clicking the perfect beat, and her smile wide and bright. Kristin really did not feel like dealing with her, not that day. Eliza tried every day to make Kristin miserable.

Elizabeth noticed Kristin seemed to be distracted. She asked, "What are you looking at?"

"Eliza. She's heading our–" Kristin was caught off by Eliza.

"Hey, Elizabeth!" Eliza exclaimed. Her clique was with her, Nicole, Priscilla, Jennifer, Danielle, and Olivia.

Kristin examined Eliza's outfit: a classic Burberry checker print shirt tucked into a black mini skirt. Kristin thought she recognized the skirt from the racks of Saks, but she couldn't quite remember. Eliza was wearing black tights and Chanel two-tone riding boots. Kristin felt like a homeless woman compared to Eliza on that day. She also spotted four gold Cartier LOVE bracelets stacked on Eliza's wrist. She mentally rolled her eyes. How come it seemed like Eliza had everything Kristin wanted? Times four.

Eliza smiled phony.

"Hey," Elizabeth greeted.

Eliza dumped her books into Nicole's hands, and she and Elizabeth hugged. Usually, Elizabeth was cold towards Eliza. After all, the way Eliza had broken off their friendship was brutal. Not to mention the fact that she rubbed it in their face every day. Kristin wondered what made her want to be nice to Eliza all of a sudden. All Kristin could do was stand there in amazement.

When they pulled away from their hug, Eliza glanced over at Kristin. "Oh, hey Kristin, I didn't see you standing there," Eliza said. She smiled phonily.

Kristin saw straight through it. "Oh, please," Kristin muttered.

She looked down at her shoes. "Actually, you're right. No one could miss that outfit. Aren't those jeans from last season? My maid probably even has them," Eliza said laughing. Her robot friends all laughed too. Kristin could have sworn she saw Elizabeth crack a smile. What was going on today? Everything was going south. And fast.

Kristin fired back, "Whatever. Can you leave? We don't want to talk to you."

"That's where you're wrong, Krissy," Eliza said, "You might not want to talk to me, but Lizzie does. I actually came over here to ask Elizabeth something, not you. Elizabeth, do you want to hang out after school today? We're all going to Nicole's house. They're finishing up renovations at mine today, thank God. Nicole's house is so *small*."

Nicole spoke up, "It's 5,000 square feet."

"Like I said, it's *small*. Anyway, you wanna come? We're having Mexican, your favorite," Eliza urged in a persuasive voice. Kristin's eyes darted to Elizabeth, who seemed to actually be considering it. She had to say something. She couldn't let her best friend hang out with her ex-best friend. That was a setup for a ton of drama, and she had enough of that in her life.

"Are you seriously going to hang out with her? Come on, Elizabeth, you have to be smarter than that," Kristin said. She did not even care that Eliza was standing right there.

"Why do you even care? We're not even friends," Elizabeth pointed out. She turned to Eliza and said, "I'll be there."

"Great. Walk with me to gym class. By the way, I love your hair today," Eliza said. She ran her fingers through Elizabeth's dirty blond locks. The two girls linked arms and walked off. Just as they were walking, the bell rang. Kristin went to her lockers and grabbed her gym clothes. She was raging with fury. How could Elizabeth betray her like that? Eliza was and always was going to be the enemy. Couldn't Elizabeth see that Eliza was only trying to create more of a rift between Kristin and Lizzie? She was excited to get to gym class to release some of her fury.

Once everyone had finished changing into their gym clothes, they walked onto the gym floor. Kristin sported her usual Lululemon attire, Elizabeth opted for a plain T-shirt and shorts, and Eliza was wearing a designer track suit. All the students sat in a circle, while Coach Williams took attendance and put them on teams. Kristin was on the red team, and Lizzie was on the blue team with Eliza. That was perfect. The only thing on Kristin's mind was getting Elizabeth's whole team out, except for Elizabeth. Looking across the gym, she watched Elizabeth chat it up with Eliza and her crew. She just could not understand why Eliza had to always make everything ten times worse. Kristin did not want them to catch her standing all alone, so she walked over to one of her friends–Stacey. Stacey had been friends with Kristin since she had first transferred to Eldridge. The girls were much closer when they were younger. They were constantly playing together and having sleepovers. As time passed, both went their separate ways. No matter what, they could always pick up from right where they left off. Out the corner of her eye, Kristin saw Elizabeth looking at her. Kristin pretended not to see her, and continued on with her conversation with Stacey about Stacey's big move to a new house. Kristin was even enjoying the talk a little, when Coach Williams blew his whistle. Kristin put her hands to her eyes and shut her eyes really quickly. That whistle had to be the loudest, most obnoxious whistle on the planet.

Coach Williams explained the rules and object of the game. It had to have been the tenth time the class had played it already. He was going to bring out all the dodgeballs, and the students were to disperse them throughout the gym. When you were hit by a ball–you were out, you were to sit down against the wall. There was to be no over aggressiveness or competiveness. Above all, there was to be no throwing balls above the waist. Coach Williams repeated for what seemed like the hundredth time that if anyone was seen breaking the rules, they'd be sent to the office and severely punished. The game would end when an entire team was out.

Within a few minutes, the game had started. The gym was filled with loud screams and yelling. Kristin found herself ducking and jumping to avoid balls every few seconds. At the same time, she was throwing balls as fast as she could. She was in her zone. It was almost as if the whole world was slowing down, or at least that is how it felt. The entire time she kept thinking about finally throwing the ball at Elizabeth. Kristin could not wait to see the look on her face. Time passed quickly. Soon, there were only three people left on Elizabeth's side; Elizabeth, Eliza, and Samantha Roche, who looked like she was going to pass out from an anxiety attack any minute. Almost everyone on Kristin's side was still in, including Kristin herself. Soon, Samantha was out. Balls began flying towards Elizabeth and Eliza, and they both ran around trying to avoid them. With all the flying balls and chaos, Eliza managed to get out of the gym; she told Coach Williams she had a bathroom emergency. Kristin didn't notice Eliza was gone until a minute later.

Then, it happened. It came so fast that she did not even see it coming. In fact, no one did. It just sort of came out of nowhere. A ball flew toward Elizabeth extremely fast, and hit her in the head. The large ball smacked the side of her head. Elizabeth's petite body fell from the large impact. Everyone on Kristin's side stopped moving and dropped their balls. The students who were already out ran back onto the court. Someone went to notify Coach Williams, who was in his office. Students surrounded her body. Kristin was also in the crowd of people. She tried to push through the people and get to her friend. Every kid was whispering something different. Elizabeth's eyes were closed. Her body was completely still. She sure did not look like she would be okay.

Coach Williams ran over to the scene and cleared everyone out. Kristin stood back with Stacey.

Coach Williams began to lightly shake Elizabeth and say her name. She didn't move. Kristin felt her heart plummet. Instead of standing there, she did the first thing that came to mind. She ran to the office.

Kristin spotted the secretary, Mrs. Owens. Mrs. Owens greeted Kristin. "How may I help you?"

"We need you to call the ambulance. Elizabeth Showers fell and she's hurt. She's unconscious."

Mrs. Owens asked, "Which student is it that's hurt, again?"

Kristin quickly said, "Elizabeth Showers. Please hurry, Mrs. Owens. She's not moving!"

"Don't worry, Kristin. I'll call the EMS right now. Why don't you go back into the gym, sweetie?"

Kristin left the office and went back to the gym. Everything was happening so quickly. Elizabeth was still lying on the floor, and Coach Williams was still shaking her. Was that all the man could think of? Wasn't he supposed to be trained to handle these sorts of situations? "Elizabeth are you okay? Elizabeth wake up. Elizabeth! Elizabeth! She might have a concussion. This is going to take a long incident report," said Coach Williams.

"All you can think about is an incident report?" Kristin asked. "Wow! That's my best friend."

Eliza butted in, "Technically, she *was* your best friend."

"Not now, Eliza."

Ten minutes later, the ambulance team walked into the gym with a stretcher. Tension filled the air as they performed the standard procedure on Elizabeth. They carried Elizabeth to a stretcher. Kristin, Coach Williams, and all of the other students watched solemnly. Kristin could not believe the way the day was going so far. At that point, she was almost sure that things couldn't get any worse. In seconds the ambulance was carrying her out of the gym. The guilt was eating Kristin up alive. Why had she had that big fight with Elizabeth? Why had she done what she had done? Then she remembered, Elizabeth was selfish. In a sense, she got what she deserved.

All through the day, Kristin had only one person on her mind, Elizabeth. She couldn't help thinking about what she had just done to her, what she had put her through. As soon as school officially let out at 3:00 p.m., Coach Williams approached her. Kristin was standing by her locker, packing up her backpack. The only thing on her mind was getting out of that school. Lucky for her, her mother was picking her up early that day. Kristin could tell by the way Coach Williams was walking that something serious was on his mind. His usually pleasant face was tight and a little scary.

"Hi, Kristin. How are you? You still must be upset about what happened to Elizabeth," said Coach Williams.

"I am. I feel kind of bad," Kristin said, "I feel terrible about what I've done to her. This whole thing is just a mess... I really wanna visit her, but after everything that happened, I don't know if I can."

Coach Williams raised his eyebrow at her words. Kristin could tell he seemed to be processing her words.

Coach Williams replied heartily, "Oh, I'm sure everything will be fine. Do you think you'll be okay?"

"Yeah, I'll be fine, I just keep thinking about it. When your best friend is sent to the hospital, it kind of has a toll on you." She loudly exhaled. "But, I'm all about positive thinking, so I'm sure she's fine."

"Oh, well I'm sure you'll find out soon," the coach said, "The principal knows that Elizabeth is a person who is liked by most people, but he also knows that Elizabeth is very fortunate, and that there may be some people who were "out to get her." I'm sure whoever it was didn't plan for her to be in the hospital now, though. Anyway, do you

41

have a few minutes Kristin? Principal Edwards wants to talk with you."

Kristin replied, "Yes, I do. My mom can wait a few minutes. She's probably not even here yet, knowing her."

Kristin followed Coach Williams into the office and took a seat. Coach Williams must have wanted to talk to Principal Edwards alone. He stepped into Principal Edward's private office and closed the door. Kristin was trying her best to keep calm. It wasn't working. Her body was shaking a bit. She hated being questioned, by anybody, especially a principal. She saw one of the school's nerdiest kids, Paul, in the office. She wondered what on earth had landed him in the office. She could hear loud yelling coming out of Principal Edwards' office. Kristin was about to spark up a conversation with him, when Coach Williams exited. His face was tomato red, his jaws were tightly clenched, and his fists were balled. Angrily, he marched out the office. She was going to ask him if he was okay, when Principal Edwards motioned for her to come into his office.

"How are you Kristin?" asked the principal.

"I'm fine."

Principal Edwards nodded and said, "I see. I'm just going to ask you a few questions. But before you answer any of them, know that you are a suspect and to tell you the truth, the only suspect. Everything you say will be documented but, you are also innocent until proven guilty."

Kristin couldn't believe Principal Edwards. What was this, a courtroom? She thought she was just coming in to talk about it. She did not know she was the suspect. Kristin burst out laughing.

"That, Mr. Edwards, is too funny. Who are you now, Judge Judy? What a knee-slapper," she said while slapping her knee and laughing uncontrollably.

"Kristin, I do not see anything funny whatsoever. You are being very disrespectful right now."

Kristin tried to regain her composure. "I find it funny that you think I did it. I don't want to sit here and be accused of giving a classmate a concussion, not to mention the fact that she is my best friend. I think I'll leave." She got up from her seat and headed for the door.

"If you leave now, I'll just write up your expulsion and then you can leave," the principal said. "You walking out is basically like you saying that you did do it, and you just want to get it over with. Students are not going to be friends with someone they think is a bully. But, if you prove them wrong, they'll be on your side." Principal Edwards paused and then continued, "What do you want to do? It's your choice. Now, I'm on your side. But there's someone who thinks that you are definitely guilty. So, sit back down and listen."

Kristin slowly walked back to her seat.

"How was your relationship with Elizabeth before she received her concussion? You two were friends, I take it."

"Well...You can say we weren't really on speaking terms. We had a big fight at my house yesterday. She was really mad; a little *too* mad if you ask me. She stormed out of the house."

Principal Edwards looked at Kristin, thinking she might be guilty. "What else happened during the fight?"

43

"I told her that I was sorry. Then, she totally went off on me. Today at her locker, things only got worse."

"Okay. What are some traits of Elizabeth?" asked Principal Edwards.

"Hmm. Selfish, party pooper, spoiled. I guess I'm a little bias, though, right?" Kristin found it a little odd that he was asking her all these questions. She tried her best to disregard it and looked at the clock on Principal Edwards' wall. In ten minutes, American Studies would be starting. She sighed.

Principal Edwards was writing something down on a notepad. Kristin noticed it. If she was going to fight the battle of being a suspect, she had to be on her toes, and seem more confident than she really was. "What you writing, Mr. Edwards?" she asked curiously.

"Nothing, just...jotting down what I need from the grocery store."

Kristin found her name on the paper. This was definitely not a grocery list, definitely. "A grocery list that has *my* name on it, Principal Edwards? Really?"

He swallowed, but didn't reply. He changed the subject. "Let's say you did do this to Elizabeth...what would you get out of it?" he asked.

"Nothing, nothing at all. Maybe, a little bit of satisfaction, but that's about it. But, what would that really solve? Within a week, she'd be back. Right? Plus, we're taking her limo to the mall next weekend, and we have to be friends by then."

He nodded, trying to seem like he understood.

Truthfully, he was confused. Here was the daughter of a parent he was friends with sitting in his office, and he might have to suspend her. "Could you say that you are kind of sick of Elizabeth?"

Kristin took a minute, and moved her hair from her face. She studied Edwards. He had a few wrinkles, a long nose, but it wasn't pointy. She noticed how his lips were a little round, and right now they were tightly closed. His hair looked a mess. He only had a little hair left in the center of his head, and it was dyed a jet black color. Kristin desperately wanted to give that man a makeover. Even so, some things about his appearance could never be changed. He barely had a neck at all. It was like his head and shoulders were one. To be honest, he was an oddly proportioned man. "Not exactly sick of her, just annoyed. Sometimes we have little fights, but I've never exactly felt like this during a fight." There was a silent pause, and then Kristin spoke up again, "So, what's next? Are you going to suspend me? Because, that won't help you. You'll still have a student in the hospital. And, if you suspend me, my mom will make sure that this school's highly valued reputation goes to shambles. You'll lose $20,000 in tuition. And you don't want that, do you, Principal Edwards? Do you? I mean, you still have to pay for your Lamborghini, right?"

Principal Edwards said calmly, "My transportation has nothing to do with this. And, if getting a girl out of this school who I think is dangerous is going to cost $20,000, I'll do it."

Kristin was shocked by his stinging comment. Kristin sat there and glanced at the clock above his head.

"I cannot suspend you, yet," he continued, "I need to get some witnesses. But you watch yourself, Kristin, do you hear me?"

"I hear you. Is that all?" she asked. She folded her arms and tapped her foot.

"Yes. You can go now."

Kristin walked out the office and saw Eliza standing against the wall next to the door. One of her feet was against the wall. Eliza was looking at her reflection in a mini mirror and adjusting her hair. She snapped it shut when Kristin walked out. "Hey, Kris," she said. She stood right in front of Kristin, blocking her path.

Kristin was just about fed up with Eliza for the day. She wanted more than anything to snuggle up with a warm blanket, drink hot chocolate, and watch Netflix. Ah, Netflix. Netflix could cure almost anything. "Are you stalking me?" Kristin asked with a smirk. "Cause if you are, that's really weird. Just thought you should know."

"Don't flatter yourself. I just saw you go into Edwards' office, and a little before that, I heard that he was suspicious about Elizabeth's incident. I told him you might know something, and that you two had a little fight and maybe you had something to do with it."

"Stay out of it. Go find someone else to mess with."

"Nope, I like messing with you. Oh, Krissy, you're so naive. Didn't I used to call you Krissy when we were friends in pre-kindergarten?"

"Oh please, Eliza! You know that until the summer of ninth grade, you, me, and Lizzie were best friends. You make it seem like it was years ago."

"Yeah, and then I made the best decision of my life and stopped hanging out with you losers! When I was friends with you guys, I couldn't get a date if I begged for one. Now, I can get a boyfriend without even trying."

"Where's your posse?"

"How would I know? I don't go *everywhere* with them."

"Look, I'd love to chat, but–" Kristin paused and said, "Actually, who am I kidding? I don't want to talk to you for another second." She shot Eliza a disgusted look. Sometimes, it amazed her that Eliza used to be one of her closest friends. People really could change. Eliza folded her arms at Kristin's rude words. Kristin stared into Eliza's sharp, green eyes. Eliza stared back. The stare down went on for about a minute, when Kristin realized how pointless it was. "Ugh," she grumbled, before storming off. Eliza chuckled and flipped again. Once again, she had beaten Kristin.

Kristin nearly ran out of the school that day. She had never been more happy to see her mother. She embraced her mother in a tight hug. Mrs. Gregory was confused, but appreciated the affection nevertheless. She surprised her daughter, yet again, by telling her that they were going to their favorite restaurant. Kristin pretended not to be too upset about the day's events while she was in the car. She tried her best to casually talk about what was going on. That did not mean that Mrs. Gregory did not notice that something about her daughter was off. She figured it had something to do with

Elizabeth, and decided to wait until they arrived at the restaurant to talk to Kristin about it.

"So how is Elizabeth?" Mrs. Gregory asked.

Kristin looked more interested in the simple decor of the restaurant than her mother's words. She then played with the salad on her plate. She picked up a cucumber with her fork and then dropped it. Kristin stumbled over her words a little. "Um, well." She exhaled loudly and tucked a strand of hair behind her ear. "I don't really know."

Mrs. Gregory replied, "What do you mean? How can you not know?" She eyed her daughter suspiciously.

Kristin knew it was best to come clean to her mother. Besides, if there was one person who Kristin could tell anything to, it was her mother. Kristin explained the entire ordeal. Talking about it made her have to think about it all over again. As she explained how Elizabeth got hurt, she got a little emotional. Her mother reached out and touched her daughter's hand. Kristin picked up a napkin and dried her eyes quickly. She was glad that she had not put on any makeup that day. That would have been a real mess. Her mother was chewing on a french fry when Kristin also told the part about Principal Edwards threatening her.

She nearly choked. "What?" she nearly yelled. A couple of people in the restaurant eyed her. "Why would he think that *you* did it?"

"Well, we did just have a fight. And I was pretty mad. And she pretty much disowned me right before gym class," Kristin admitted.

Mrs. Gregory picked up another french fry. "Wow, I can't believe Julie didn't even call me." She thought about everything her daughter had just told her. She and Elizabeth's mother were almost as close as Kristin and Elizabeth. "Kristin, I know this going to sound crazy, but you didn't throw the ball, did you?"

This time, Kristin was the one who nearly choked on a fry. Out of all the things that had angered her that day, this was the icing on the cake. Her own mother was doubting her daughter's character.

"No, Mom! I did not knock Elizabeth out. God, first it's Edwards and now it's you." Kristin chuckled a bit. "My day keeps getting better and better. If you couldn't tell, that was sarcasm."

Her mother apologized. "I'm sorry, dear. I didn't mean it like that."

Kristin suddenly felt nauseous.

"But don't you think you should maybe call Mrs. Showers," her mother continued, "Elizabeth would like to see you, I'm sure."

"I'm sure she won't." She stood up and looked at her salad. "I'm not hungry anymore. Take me home."

The next day, Kristin walked through the doors of the school a little early. Stacey and a couple of her other friends were waiting by the door for her. They walked and talked together. A few girls approached her. A couple even asked her if she had any plans for the week, mostly about the movies that were playing in the theaters. Though Kristin was happy to know that her friends still liked her, things did not feel the same without Elizabeth. Stacey was saying something about a new horror flick, but

Kristin was consumed by the sight of Steve Sanders. Steve's eyes met hers and he winked. She was happy that her friends had not seen the small act; they never would have stopped talking about it. Once, a guy had complimented her on her hair. The girls teased her relentlessly about her "luxurious locks" for weeks. They continued talking about movies at Kristin's locker. Then, they moved on to fashion. Kristin's friends were much different than Eliza. From what Kristin could tell, they actually had a bond. They weren't her puppets and for the most part, she treated them well. There was no friend she treated better than Elizabeth, though.

"Did you guys hear that Eliza has a Cartier bracelet?" Milania squealed. She was nearly hyperventilating.

Kristin grabbed her by the shoulders to calm her down. "Chill, Milania. And yes, I saw it with my own two eyes, unfortunately."

"Guys, Edwards is walking our way," Stacey informed. She tilted her head in his direction. "I think he wants to talk to you, Kristin. I'm outta here. He scares me." Stacey power walked away. The other girls said bye to Kristin and left as well.

Principal Edwards brought very interesting news. Apparently, there was going to be an assembly within minutes. He said it was going to be informing students who had not already heard about the 'Elizabeth incident.' Kristin highly doubted there was anyone who did not know by now. When Principal Edwards asked Kristin if she had been to visit Elizabeth in the hospital, she shook her head no. As Principal Edwards' only suspect so far, Kristin looked even more guilty. He shared with her that he had spoken with Elizabeth's mother. Kristin's ears perked up. She had secretly been dying to know how Elizabeth was doing. Elizabeth's mother was very upset about the state of her daughter, naturally. She wanted the person who had thrown the ball to be suspended or even permanently expelled immediately. Since the Showers family was one of the biggest donors to the school, Mrs. Showers did not have to do much convincing. Elizabeth had suffered a concussion, and would probably have to be in the hospital another night. Kristin was happy to know that nothing serious was wrong.

"Um, well, thanks for telling me all this," Kristin said.

"You're welcome. The assembly starts in a few minutes, so hurry on down to the gym; you wouldn't want to be late," Mr. Edwards replied.

Kristin gave the sweetest smile possible.

He turned and walked in the opposite direction.

When Kristin opened her locker to put her backpack inside, she instantly saw the pictures of her and Elizabeth that hung in her locker. There were a million of them everywhere. Her favorite was the one of her and Lizzie at a zoo last year. They were standing in front of a bear cave. She stared at the picture. Lizzie's smile was huge, bright, and very genuine. She looked so happy. Kristin's smile was pretty too. Well, as pretty as it could be with those ugly braces on her teeth. Thank God she'd gotten them taken off over the summer. She loved her teeth, and couldn't stand those braces. Elizabeth had never had braces, and she did not really need them. Kristin looked around the hallway. There were no children by their lockers, so she assumed that everyone was in the gym. She glanced at herself in the mirror. Her hair was pulled back into a messy bun. She didn't have on any makeup; she just wasn't in that kind of mood. She had a lot on her mind. Kristin was wondering exactly what was happening with Elizabeth, and how serious it really was. Maybe she'd go and visit her today. Probably. She stuffed her backpack in her locker and started heading towards the gym.

Kristin looked up and noticed that Steve Sanders was walking her way. He'd been her crush since forever, but right now she wasn't even thinking about him. He seemed pretty excited to see her. He stopped her in the hall to say, hey. Plainly, she told him, hi. She knew her reply wasn't very pleasant, but she didn't really have much to be pleasant about, except for the Lianna Gibson party, which was the next day. What he said next shocked her.

"So, um, I was wondering if sometime we can hang out? You know, maybe a movie or dinner? Or both. Just anything you're up to. Or maybe we could just hang at my place," Steve said nervously.

"Yeah, that sounds fun. I would like to talk about it more but I have to get to the assembly," Kristin responded in a rushed manner.

"Oh, yeah. I forgot about the assembly thingy. Can I have your number?" He questioned.

"Yes!" Kristin said excitedly. She then tried to cover up her excitement by saying in a calm way, "I mean, sure. That'd be cool."

Steve laughed and replied, "You're funny." He continued, "Do you have any paper that you could write your number down on?"

"No, actually I don't. Shoot," she mumbled. Kristin then remembered that she had a marker in her boot. She'd been rushing to close her backpack this morning and tried to stuff everything in there. When she finally had managed to get it closed, she realized she hadn't put in the marker so decided to stuff it in her boot. "Oh, I have a marker in my boot. Is it okay if I write it on your hand?"

Steve offered out his hand and Kristin grabbed the marker out of her boot. She carefully wrote the number, trying not the let it smudge at all. It felt great holding his hand, and she felt sparks. When she finished she said, "Done."

"Thanks."

Kristin replied, "If you don't mind me asking, why'd you ask me out now? We've known each other since seventh grade."

He said, "Kristin, you've been my crush forever."

Kristin flashed a smile, and continued walking towards the gym. She couldn't believe that Steve had just asked her out. And, he asked her for her number which was even better. Maybe today wouldn't be that bad after all.

The assembly only lasted thirty minutes. It had gone better than she Kristin hoped. Principal Edwards had basically informed the school about the status of the Elizabeth situation. She did not have any bleeding of the brain, and her concussion was a pretty standard one. Doctors were still running tests on her, just to make sure everything was good. She should be back to normal within a couple days. Elizabeth's mother wanted all the students to know that Lizzie was appreciative of the get well cards and flowers. Principal Edwards mentioned that Mrs. Showers was very upset about what had happened to her daughter, naturally. Edwards had also mentioned that when he figured out who was responsible for Elizabeth's accident, they would be possibly expelled. Kristin swallowed hard when she heard that. She was not the only one in the room to be fearful. The entire school gasped at his words. Eldridge had not had to suspend or expel someone since, well, ever. The students were so prestigious, poised, and eloquent. It wasn't surprising that the school was taking this so seriously. They had a strict policy against violence, and Coach Williams had always told the students that if they ever threw a dodgeball above the waist, they would be in a lot of trouble. Kristin just never imagined the person would be in suspension or expulsion trouble.   Principal Edwards had brought an oversized get well card for the students to sign it. Elizabeth was not popular like Eliza, but she was liked pretty well by all the normal kids. She was one of the nicest and friendliest people. The entire school signed the card, except for Kristin. She just didn't feel right signing it. Kristin sat next to her friend Lucy during the assembly. Lucy sometimes hung out with Kristin and Elizabeth. Lucy and Kristin small talked for awhile, until Lucy revealed that she had visited Elizabeth in the hospital. This came as a surprise to Kristin. Lucy and Elizabeth weren't even close. Lucy told Kristin that Elizabeth was fearful about returning to school. According to

Lucy, Elizabeth was afraid that the person would try to hurt her again. Hearing this made Kristin have even more compassion for her friend. Kristin was sure that whoever had done it certainly was not out to get her. In fact, Kristin believed the incident was purely a mistake. While Principal Edwards was rambling on about violence, Lucy asked Kristin if she had been to see her friend. Kristin's response was not very truthful. She did not want to seem like a heartless monster. She claimed that she had an important family function to go to. Lucy did not entirely buy it.

Lucy said, "Oh, I see. I just thought that maybe you didn't go because of your fight."

The students who were sitting in the rows near them all turned to face Lucy and Kristin when they heard this.

Kristin said above a whisper, "Don't be so loud and how do you know about that?"

"So it's true then? Elizabeth disowned you?" Lucy wondered.

Kristin tried to dodge the question. She asked, "What else are people saying about me?"

"I don't want to upset you. You know how crazy rumors can be. And half the time they aren't even true."

"Then why do you believe the one about me and Lizzie fighting? Listen, Lucy, I love you, but my friendship problem with Elizabeth is none of your business–or anyone else's for that matter," Kristin told her.

Lucy opened her mouth to speak, but closed it. She folded her arms. The two did not speak to each other for the rest of the assembly. Kristin did not regret what she had said. Maybe that would be enough to get Lucy to stop listening to Eliza and her army. Kristin suspected they had been the ones to start the gossip.

After eight hours of horrible school, Kristin was packing up her things at her locker. She stared at her reflection in the mirror for awhile and before she knew it, Steve was right behind her.

"Don't worry, you're beautiful," he commented.

Kristin jumped at the sound of his voice. She turned around stunned and put her hand on her heart. "Gosh, you scared me. And thanks. Wait, I'm beautiful? Don't most guys usually use the word 'hot'?"

Steve said seriously, "I'm not like most guys. I'm way hotter."

Kristin did not know whether or not to take this as a joke. She thought it was a joke, but Steve's face did not look like he was joking. She tried to contain her laughter.

"I'm kidding, he finally said.

She said, "Oh." They both looked at each other and burst into laughter. Kristin covered her face. It was burning red. This was the most laughter she had gotten all day. It felt nice to be a little happy, especially talking to a guy. When they both gained their composure, there was a small awkward silence. They looked at each other for a few seconds. Kristin nervously bit her lip. What should she say next? Or should he say something next? She had not done the whole flirting thing in awhile, and even though she knew it was wrong for her to be so into Steve while her best friend was in the hospital, she couldn't help it. He was just so charming.

Steve ended up being the first one to break the silence. He asked her if she had anything planned for the afternoon. He had wanted for them to go get smoothies at a place near their school. She could tell he was a little nervous. This only added to his adorableness. How could such a good looking jock be nervous to talk to a girl? When she said yes, she could see a light sparkle in his green eyes. Yet again, her cheeks turned a rosy red color. Kristin was a little apprehensive about getting into the car with a guy she did not know all that well, but she figured nothing bad would happen. She highly doubted that Steve was a secret criminal.

"Nice car," she commented as he opened the door to his Audi coupe for her.

"Thanks."

At the coffee shop, Steve said, "So I heard that you got invited to Lianna Gibson's party. That's pretty cool."

"Yeah, my mom works at a music studio. Lianna happened to be in town, and came by the studio." "That's cool. You must have a really cool mom." "Thanks," She replied.

"My parents have cool jobs too. What does your dad do?"

Kristin swallowed hard. "He passed away."

"Oh. Gosh, I'm really screwing up. I'm sorry I asked. I am *not* good with girls, if you can't tell." "It's fine. You didn't know," Kristin assured him while laughing a little. Kristin flagged down the waitress. "Can I have a donut?" she asked.

"Sure. Now, I must warn you, it's pretty big and has a lot of calories. I know how you teenage girls are. You still want it?"

Kristin nodded.

"And for you, young man?" She looked at Steve.

"Mocha frappe, please," he replied.

The waitress hurried off.

Steve said, "You're much different than Eliza."

Kristin scrunched her eyebrows in confusion.

Steve explained, "She was my last girlfriend. She counted calories every single second."

Kristin replied, "Boy has she changed."

This time, Steve was the one to scrunch his eyebrows.

"I used to be friends with her. The Eliza I knew used to eat any and everything. Eliza has morphed into a completely new person."

The waitress came back and put their orders on the table.

"Yeah. Everything was going great between us, and then one day she told me that she felt like something was wrong between us. She hurt me so badly. I felt like I was nothing. I know it's stupid. I'm stupid."

"So was I for even being her friend. Gosh, we both sound like we're depressed." Kristin and Steve erupted in laughter.

As they stuffed themselves with carbs, Kristin said, "You're on the football team right?"

"And the basketball team. It has perks, and some of them aren't so good," Replied Steve.

"Explain to me how being able to skip classes whenever you want to and having cheerleaders in your face isn't good. Maybe I'm missing something?"

"Well," started Steve, "I don't skip class. Some of my friends do, but I think that it's stupid. Me

58

and this other guy on the football team named Josh are the only two who don't lie and say we have practice so that we can skip class. And, other than Liza, I've never dated a cheerleader. It's kind of hard to get girls when you're on the team, they have such high expectations. People automatically think that I'm a jerk because I'm a jock. Teachers don't respect us at all; people have misconceptions about us athletes. Plus, I have five hour practices, I skipped today though. I couldn't even try out for the debate team because I have a commitment to the team. And my life is not perfect, contrary to what everyone seems to think. I'm a human too."

"Wow. You totally just impressed me," Kristin stated. She folded her arms.

"You impressed me too. I haven't had this much fun with a girl in a while. I don't want to rush into anything. I just know that this was fun, and I like you. I can't wait for the Lianna Gibson thing."

"Me too. It's going to be really fun. And I can already tell that you're a really cool guy."

They continued talking for a little while. At one point, a gusty wind came and Kristin shivered. Steve took off his varsity jacket and wrapped it around her shoulders. Kristin could hardly believe the day's events. She never could have imagined she'd be talking with Steve Sanders outside of school, and that he would actually seem like he was into her. She learned that his favorite color was purple; his favorite snacks were Oreos, Swedish Fish, and Cheez Its; and he loved any TV shows that had anything to do with criminal law. Kristin checked her watch. It was nearly 6:00 p.m. Had she and Steve really been talking for that long? She wanted to tell him that she probably needed to be starting her homework, but she did not want to seem like a stick in the mud. She figured homework could wait a little. Out the corner of her eye, Kristin spotted a Burberry shirt that looked all too familiar. Eliza and her entourage approached them.

Eliza said cynically, "Well, what do we have here?"

"Nothing. We were just leaving," Steve said. He stood up, but Eliza put her hand on his chest and stopped him. He looked down at her hand, signaling her to remove it.

"I was just coming here with the girls to grab a some coffee, but I might as well kill two birds with one stone. Steve, I was wondering if you wanted to come to my party this Saturday. It's at my house. Everyone on the football team is invited, but she," Eliza sent Kristin a dirty look, "definitely is not."

"I won't be able to make it. Kristin and I are going to Lianna Gibson's birthday party this Saturday."

"Why are you even with her? She's not half as pretty as me, or rich. She's disgusting. She think she's pretty because of her designer clothes, but nothing can cover up how evil and hideous she is."

Kristin felt tears swelling in her eye.

Eliza and her friends began cackling. Their laughs sounded like those of an evil witch's and her little demons.

Kristin looked at Steve quickly, and then got up from her seat. She ran away from the table. She began approaching Steve's car. Soon, Steve was running towards her. Kristin hid her face in her hands, embarrassed that she had run away and let Eliza win. She felt like the biggest idiot for even letting Eliza get in her head.

"Kristin, you okay?" Steve rushed to her side and put his hand lightly on her shoulder. She flinched instinctively and he removed his hand. An awkward silence filled the crisp air. Seconds went by, until Kristin finally gained the strength to speak up.

She asked, "Can we leave? I've got homework."

"I'm sorry she came and messed everything up. I swear I didn't know she was going to do that. I'm so sorry, Kristin."

Kristin replied through tears, "Thanks for your pity, but take me home now."

Without replying, Steve opened the car door for her and closed it. As they were driving he commented, "What happened was neither of our faults. I know how mean Liza is but, even though you were mad, you can't just, you know, run away."

Kristin snapped, "I didn't run away. You don't even know me. Back off. I shouldn't even be in a car with you. You might try to kidnap me." Suddenly, she became defensive. Steve knew nothing about her and Eliza's past. Hearing about betrayal was much different than living through it. No one understood what it was like to lose a best friend, someone you imagined being your maid-of-honor.

He disagreed. "Calm down," he said, "no one is trying to kidnap you. Just don't be afraid of her. Who cares if she calls you a loser?"

Kristin questioned, "So you're calling me a loser?"

"No, no, no. That's not what I meant at all."

"Just leave me alone. I'm done with this conversation," she muttered. It was not until the nasty words had escaped her mouth that she realized the way she sounded. The more she thought about it, the more she realized how much she sounded like Eliza. Kristin mentally punched herself. Pride kept her from apologizing. That, along with the fact that she was still a little ticked off.

When he pulled up to her house she thanked him quietly. As she was about to go inside the house, Steve yelled from the car, "Wait!"

Kristin stopped dead in her tracks and turned around. She yelled back, "What?"

Quickly, Steve jumped out of his car. He was making his way towards her. He stopped when he was a few feet away. "Did you ever consider that maybe I asked you out because I really *like* you? Did you ever? You know what? I don't even want to go to Lianna's party, not with someone who doesn't trust anyone. You have way too many issues that I do not need in my life."

Kristin stood at the door speechless.

Steve shook his head before walking to his car and driving off. Maybe he was right. Maybe suddenly Kristin did not trust people. She slowly dragged her backpack up the stairs.

Her mother said from the kitchen, "Kristin, where were you? I was supposed to pick you up from school. I waited there for an hour; I texted you and called you a million times."

"I went to go get coffee, Mom. Sorry, I won't do it again. I'm just really not feeling like talking right now, so I'm going to my room."

"You didn't take your car; how'd you get there?"

"I went with Steve, and *he* has a car," Kristin responded with anger.

"Okay, Kris. I'll bring dinner to your room in a couple of hours, sweetie. Just make sure you do all of your homework, okay?"

"Yes, Mom," Kristin muttered.

Kristin struggled with her math homework in her room. It was this one problem that was giving her trouble. Gosh, she could have really used Elizabeth a time like this. She spent ten minutes staring at the problem, and redid it millions of times. Finally, she realized her mistake, checked her new answer in the back of the book, and moved on to the next problem. After forty minutes, she was done with math. It had felt more like four hours. Now, on to English. She had to read four chapters of a new book by next Wednesday, and do the study questions that were online. She was not the fastest reader. These study questions counted as a grade, so she reread every chapter twice. She was in chapter two when her phone rang. Kristin saw Lucy's face appear on the screen.

"Hello?" Kristin answered.

"Go to Eliza's MyPage right now. This is a 911!"

Kristin muttered, "Um, all right," as she picked up her laptop, she quickly typed in the website's name. "Almost to the site." After a few seconds, she said, "Okay, I'm here. What's Eliza's MyPage name?"

Lucy said with annoyance in her voice, "MissBeautifulLiza. No spaces."

A few seconds passed. "Oh my gosh." She scrolled through Eliza's most recent posts. Eliza had somehow recorded and taken pictures of the incident at the cafe. Kristin ran her hand through her hair. "Why would she do this to me? I'm scared to watch the video." Kristin reluctantly pressed play, and watched her horrible moment with Eliza over again. She even saw the part where she ran off. It was horrible. While watching the video, she heard something she had not heard the first time. As soon as Kristin had run off, Steve said, "Eliza, what's your problem? Gosh, why would you say that?" Turns out he had defended her against Eliza. Eliza must have had one of her friends filming them. The entire thing had been a dirty set-up, and he had stuck up for her. She scrolled down, and skimmed some of the comments. She had never read so many disgusting things about herself. People she thought were her friends were calling her names and making fun of her.

Lucy was on the other end asking, "Are you there?"

Kristin felt paralyzed. She hated to seem dramatic, but she felt like her life was falling to pieces. Kristin then remembered Lucy. "That's it. I'm calling Eliza right now," Kristin announced.

"Good luck, Kristin." She heard the phone click. Okay, now all she needed to do was call Eliza–no big deal. Not at all. It was just Eliza; she had known her for years. She had just seen her that same day. It's not like Eliza was Kim Kardashian. She was just an ordinary girl, right?

As Kristin dialed the number she knew so well, she started running through all of the memories from the years. Kristin was still trying to muster up the courage to press the Call button on her phone. She remembered when she and Eliza both dressed up as angels when they were little for Halloween. Every single Halloween, they were angels together. Kristin then thought about the time when they would blast music from Kristin's stereo, and do cheesy dance moves. Neither one of them was very good at dancing, but they would always pretend. They even made a dance tutorial video and put it on the Internet. It only got 100 views, but they were very happy with it. She, Eliza and Elizabeth would always play hide and go seek in the basement of Eliza's house. They'd wait until it got dark, and then they would start the game. The girls would go to the beach together. They would even volunteer at local soup kitchens together, even though Eliza really didn't like labor.

Then she remembered the summer of ninth grade. Eliza started caring so much about her makeup and hair that she forgot her friends. She was hanging out with popular people, going to pool parties, in which she would strut skimpy, designer bikinis, with the in crowd. She was shutting Elizabeth and Kristin out, no matter how hard they tried to bring the old Eliza back. Eventually, Elizabeth and Kristin stopped chasing after her, and decided to give up. The whole thing was plain exhausting. As Kristin struggled to press the Call button, she thought of how she and Eliza used to talk on the phone for hours. Soon, the phone began ringing. It went straight to voicemail. Kristin sighed; she was a little relieved. This feeling was short-lived, because nearly instantly Eliza called back.

"Hello?" Kristin asked. One of her nails was in

her mouth.

"Who's this and why'd you call my phone?" Eliza asked.

There was annoyance in her voice.

"It's Kristin."

Eliza said, "Eww. What do you want?"

"Why did you post all of that nasty stuff about me?" Kristin demanded. She figured that jumping straight to the point was probably the best option. No need to make a useless attempt at small-talk.

"Because you deserve it," Eliza explained.

"*No,*" Kristin thought, "*you deserve it.*" Instead, she said, "You're the one who hurt me!"

Eliza avoided replying to Kristin's previous statement. Instead, she replied, "Shut up. If you don't leave Steve alone, I'll make sure that everyone in the school hates you. Don't ever talk to Steve, text, or call him. Do you want to be friendless forever?"

"No," Kristin replied.

"So you're going to leave Steve alone, right?" Eliza asked.

For a moment—the smallest of moments—Kristin considered it. Then, she completely changed her mind.

"No, I'm sorry but I like him. Maybe you were stupid for dumping him."

"Fine, but just know that every chance I have to embarrass you, I will. By the way, he's a jerk."

Kristin heard the phone click signaling that Eliza had hung up.

Kristin forgot all about visiting Elizabeth in the hospital. She saw, **One New Message**, appear on her laptop. Someone had messaged her on MyPage. It was Steve!

The message read:

SteveSanders - I don't know what to say except for sorry.

Kristin looked at the message and sighed. As much as she wanted to say something, she was sure that she'd messed things up with Steve. He probably thought she was a freako now. He messaged her more.

SteveSanders - Will you talk to me?

SteveSanders - You can call me.

SteveSanders - r u there?

SteveSanders - r u mad?

SteveSanders - Should I text u?

She ignored his continuous messages, and started reading from her book again. After reading five chapters twice, she put the book on her desk. At least she had a good start on that. Now she needed to do her history homework.

Forty-five minutes into her history, her mother called from the kitchen, "Kristin, maybe you should come down for dinner. I don't think you should eat in your room."

"Okay, I'm coming down."

Over dinner, Kristin's mother asked, "So, who's Steve?"

Kristin played with the salmon on her plate. Surprisingly, it was edible. Actually, it was great. Kristin forced herself to take bites. Despite the fact that it was good, she could not bring herself to eat much. When Kristin told her how amazing he was, she saw her mother get excited. That excitement faded once she told her what happened at the cafe.

She started to tell her mother about the videos Eliza had posted, but she knew her mother would only blow the situation up. The last thing Kristin needed was her mother storming into the school making threats to Eliza.

Her mother urged her to make amends with Steve, but Kristin explained that her pride was preventing her from doing that. "Fine, but one day you're going to realize that you missed out on a good thing," her mother said, "I remember what the guys in high school were like, and there were not too many who were actually nice guys."

Her mother's words resonated with her. From prior experience, she knew that her mother was right. As Cher from *Clueless* had once said, high school boys could be like dogs. They were not like middle school boys, in the fact that they had a small amount of body muscle and their voices were no longer squeakier than a five year old. However, they were not yet like college guys; most high school boys had no clue how to be a good boyfriend. All they were looking for was a quick hookup with a girl that was just as clueless as they were. There were, however, some diamonds in the rough, and Kristin felt like Steve could potentially be one of those diamonds.

Out of nowhere, Kristin's mother asked, "Why didn't you visit Elizabeth today?"

Kristin dropped her fork. "We're not friends, why would I?"

Her mother said, "Just because you have one fight with your friend, doesn't mean that the friendship is over. You guys are like sisters, Kristin. At least visit her or call the hospital or–"

The phone began ringing. Saved by the bell, thank the Lord. Their house phone began ringing. Mrs. Gregory shot Kristin a look, as if saying *This isn't over,* and went to answer the phone from the kitchen counter. "Gregory residence," she recited eloquently. "May I ask who's calling?" She said, "Oh, Steve Sanders." She peeped her head into the dining room and smiled excitedly at Kristin. Kristin put her head in her hands. "Well, right now Kristin's eating her dinner, but I'll tell her you called." A few more seconds passed. "I will definitely pass on the message. Bye, sweetie." Returning to the table Mrs. Gregory said, "He just wants to talk to you. He sounded so...sad, Kristin. I think he cares about you."

"I'm going upstairs."

"You barely touched the asparagus and mashed potatoes. Kristin, you have to eat," her mother said.

"I'll eat it later, Mom."

Chapter 3
Party

About five minutes before school, Kristin stood at her locker re-reading her history essay. She needed to get a good grade on this essay. Maybe then, her mother would buy her that new handbag that she wanted. She saw her friend Portia Foster walking up to her locker and decided to go say hi. Portia was one of those girls who was born into a life of luxury and little hard work. She had her own saddle ranch, and her father owned twenty malls across the country. This meant that Portia had access to all the latest clothes. Portia had the beauty of a supermodel. Anyone could tell that Portia was a very fortunate child. Despite this, she was not considered popular.

"Hey, Portia," Kristin greeted. Portia never looked up from her phone. Kristin assumed that she had not heard her. She repeated the words again. When Portia still did not say anything, Kristin repeated the words louder. She waved her hands in Portia's face.

Portia grabbed Kristin's flinging arms and looked around, seeing that a few people were looking at them. She whispered, "Stop being so loud. People are staring."

Kristin laughed. She said, "Okay, okay. You act like you're embarrassed to be talking to me."

Portia stared at the ground without saying a word.

Things suddenly became clear to Kristin. Portia was embarrassed to be friends with her. Kristin said solemnly, "I thought we were friends."

"We are, but if I hang out with you, I won't have any friends at all." Portia reached out and hugged Kristin.

Kristin stood there motionless. Kristin realized that no matter how much people hated Eliza, they always were going to choose Eliza over her. Eliza was stealing all her friends.

Portia continued, "By the way, you can't come to my party tonight. No losers or wannabes invited. Sorry."

Kristin opened her mouth wide to respond, but was shocked. She was not a loser. She was a C-lister. She, Elizabeth and Portia were good examples of C-listers. They usually hung out with other C-Listers, B-Listers, and maybe if they were lucky, they even hung out with A-listers. Even though they hung out with A-listers sometimes, they could never be A-listers unless all of the A-listers officially adopted them. Maddie Lang was a B-Lister. Although she was Eliza's cousin and usually hung out with Eliza and her friends, she would sometimes hang with Kristin. Maddie had known Kristin ever since she came to the school.

They'd hung out all of the time. Maddie was a good person, and although Kristin was not as close with Maddie as she was with Elizabeth, they were kind of close. Eliza had never been too happy about Maddie remaining friends with Kristin after Eliza had ditched her.

She replied to Portia, "Fine." She was tired of hearing Portia's lies. She walked back to her locker and picked up a textbook. School was almost about to start. Kristin turned away to walk to class, but collided with a person. She backed away and rubbed her eyes. She was shocked to find that the mystery person was Steve.

Before she could think of a way to avoid the awkward situation, he spoke. He said, "I'm really sorry. I know was a jerk."

Hearing those words made Kristin melt. She then remembered Eliza's threatening words from their phone call. Maybe it would be a bad idea after all to go against Eliza, especially since Kristin was not very powerful at the moment. Eliza had already gotten revenge on Kristin by spreading the rumor about Kristin that she'd thrown the ball at Elizabeth. She would continue getting revenge if Kristin didn't leave Steve alone. She knew there was only one thing to do, if she wanted to live a semi-pleasant life. "I don't think things between us will work out, Steve."

Steve's face kind of frowned and then he said, "But I really like you. And not just your physical appearance. I *like* you."

"I know," she quickly said, "It's just timing. Right now, my life is a little crazy. I don't want to put you through that. You don't deserve it," she explained. Out the corner of her eye, she saw Eliza at the end of the hallway. She glared at Kristin and Steve.

"But, Kristin," Steve said while moving closer to her, "I really–"

Kristin blocked his body away from hers and stepped back. "Just go," she pleaded. First, she saw sadness fill his eyes. Then, she saw confusion. She folded her arms and looked away, hoping those actions would signal Steve to finally walk away. When he did not budge, she said, "Fine. I'll go. I'm almost late for Biology, anyway." As Kristin walked down the hall, she passed Eliza, who was walking in the opposite direction. Before Kristin turned the hall, she stopped. She saw Eliza reaching towards Steve, obviously trying to console him. The two began conversing. The halls were so loud that she could not make out the words. She sighed, before continuing to her class.

When she walked in the door, all eyes turned to her. She had always said how nice it would be to have all eyes on you; she just never guessed it would happen under those circumstances. The room got a little quieter, but small whispers could be heard. After she took a seat, Steve entered the room. Kristin busied herself with the pencil that was on her desk. She could feel Steve's eyes on her, which made the situation even more awkward. She had never been more grateful when her teacher entered the room and started their lesson. Kristin tried to enjoy the awful power point lecture on genetic engineering. She took the most, neat notes she had ever taken, and figured that if the rest of her life was chaotic, something in her life should be neat and put together.

Lunchtime could not come soon enough for Kristin. As she entered the dining hall seating area, she looked around for a place to sit. As she soon as she would walk towards a table filled with her friends, one of the girls would put their feet in the empty chair. Was everyone turning on her? She felt like she was in a bad dream. How could things change so drastically in such a small amount of time? All her "friends" stared at her as she walked to an empty table. Soon enough, all the students were laughing at her. Many pointed and whispered. Trying to ignore them, Kristin pulled her phone out of her back pocket and starting listening to music. But not even Miley Cyrus' *Party In the USA* could help Kristin ignore Eliza's loud laughter.

Five minutes later, Eliza stood on top of a table.

Kristin looked up from the bagel she was trying to pick with. "*Who stands on a table?*" Kristin thought.

"Attention! Attention! I just wanted to inform everyone that Kristin Gregory is sitting by herself today. The poor girl couldn't even find herself a seat. Even the geeks don't want to talk to her!" The whole cafeteria started cracking up. Kristin spotted some of her friends laughing hysterically. Eliza continued, "Isn't that tragic? That's what she deserves for giving her ex-best friend a concussion! *I* wouldn't even do that! Hopefully, she gets expelled so I'll never have to look at her ugly, fat and annoying face! Raise your hand if you agree." Nearly every hand in the room was up. Kristin looked around, embarrassed. Eliza continued, "How about we all name some things that we don't like about Kristin? Anyone want to take a shot?"

A ninth grader stood up and said, "I invited her to my Halloween party, and she told me that she'd rather go trick-or-treating with bratty three year olds. I think she's really mean, and deserves all of this hate! Isn't that how Karma works? Give hate and get hate back."

Another girl stood. "I wore some vintage jeans last year to school and asked her what she thought of them. Kristin told me that they looked ugly on me, and I should start a diet."

Ten hate comments later, a guy stood. "I asked her out on a date to go golfing. She said yes and then never showed up. I never understood why she would do that. But, she's evil."

Kristin tried hard not to cry. Why would people say all of those mean things about her? Sure, some of it was true but she had not intended to be mean...it had just sort of come out that way.

Finally Eliza said, "That's enough, guys. We wouldn't want Kristin to actually start *crying*. If you want to share some more comments and stories, go to my MyPage account dedicated to showing Kristin how much we hate her. The account name is Hate4Kristin, with the number four. No spaces. Friend me, and join the club. This has been an Eliza Parker announcement! Enjoy the rest of your lunch." As Eliza sat down, everyone starting clapping and then went back to normal conversation.

Kristin put her hands over her eyes, and breathed deeply. Silently, she began weeping. For a second, she completely forgot that she was in public. She removed her hands and saw Steve walking toward her with his lunch in his hands. He slowly sat down next to her.

"Can I sit down?" he asked cautiously.

Kristin nodded and wiped her eyes. She was embarrassed beyond belief, but also vulnerable.

He said, "I'm so sorry about all of this. Let's get out of here."

Kristin and Steve sat inside of Steve's car. At first, she had been apprehensive to leave school, but anything was better than having all those people stare, laugh, and whisper. And although she hated admitting it, she felt comfortable with Steve, he was a pretty good listener. While Kristin rambled about how spiteful Eliza was, he listened. While she cried a little and complained about how she wished things could go back to normal, he listened. He listened for a good thirty minutes, until they both realized lunch was almost over. Kristin said, "Thank you so much. I'm so sorry for being so mean to you. Eliza made it clear that if I didn't cut all ties to you, my life would be miserable. And now it is. It can't get any worse."

"I will handle that situation, I promise. Everything will be okay," he promised. He put his hand on Kristin's shoulder.

"Doesn't seem like it. I can't even eat. I miss Elizabeth to death. On top of that, I'm going to get suspended. I love this school. If I leave, what will I have? Nothing! No friends, nothing! I'll have to go to some poor public school for the rest of the year because no reputable private school will accept once the news breaks of what happens. It'll take all of about fifteen minutes for those mothers to start calling one another and relaying the news. It's not like they have anything else to do. Their careers consist of lounging at country clubs and shopping."

Steve felt bad for Kristin. Although it seemed petty for someone to be sobbing because people were gossiping about them, Steve understood that words could affect you. Half of the people who were trashing her did not truly know her. They were just pretending to feel a certain way because Eliza felt like that. Eliza was the one who truly hated Kristin. Eliza was the one with the boys following her, the crew watching her every move, the one with real popularity. She was queen, and not even Kristin would be able to touch that–ever. So why had Kristin tried to do that all of these years? It had not really worked out. She didn't have crowded weekends filled with parties and social events, and lunches with the girls. She had nail appointments, sometimes a movie night with her friends. Kristin was boring compared to Eliza. Steven put his hand over hers. "I am going to be your friend."

"Thank you. I appreciate that, but what about Maddie, my friend Maya, Penelope, Elizabeth who is most important, Cameron, Camilla, Mollie, Elaine, Veronica, Beth, and all of those people?"

"Just talk to them, Kristin. If you mean something to them, they will come to their senses," he replied.

Kristin nodded her head and sniffled. As she sat there, she came to a realization like no other. All of the bad things that were happening to her were just payback for the way she had treated people. What was the point of it all? Wanting to be popular had made her say things she never thought she would say. It had made her choose a celebrity over her friend. None of that mattered anymore. What mattered to her was getting her life in order and becoming a better person. She knew it would not be easy, but things that are worth achieving never are. Steve had convinced her to skip the rest of school. At first, she was reluctant. She had never skipped. Then, she realized that it was not a bad idea after all. It's not like Steve was going to kidnap her. The worst that could happen was that she would be a little behind on homework. They made plans to go to Steve's house to get something to eat and then hang out at his house. Kristin asked, "You can cook?" She raised one of her eyebrows.

"Not a bit, but I have a chef at home."

"A chef—I could get used to that," Kristin said while smiling. She checked herself out in the mirror. Her blue-mirror sunglasses really worked nicely with her beautiful brown hair. They had been in the car for awhile, so she decided to listen to music. She put in her ear buds and blasted her music. She snuck a quick peek at Steve. Gosh, did he always look good? He made putting on his turn signal look hot. "Friends! Friends! Friends!" She reminded herself. A smile arose on her face, as the tunes played in her ear. Two sappy love songs later, she removed her earphones. "What city do you live in?" She questioned.

"Bloomfield Hills. We should be there in fifteen minutes. Why? Getting bored with me already?" He fake gasped and put his hand on his heart, pretending to be hurt.

Kristin burst into laughter. "Hey, don't laugh at

my pain!" he said dramatically.

She said just as dramatically, "I give you my deepest apologies."

He sighed in relief. "I'm not going to get you in trouble for skipping, am I? I guess that kind of skipped my mind at the moment. I just knew that staying in school was not a good idea," he explained.

"Well, when I tell my mom that I was with the son of Michael Sanders, she'll probably be more forgiving. She likes your dad a lot. She wants to start her music company one day. She admires that your dad started off as a lawyer's assistant, and then he went and got a law degree. Next thing you know, he's the owner of the largest law firm in the Midwest." Kristin looked up from her phone and noticed that they were turning onto a street she did not recognize. She felt like she was in a different world. Not even Eliza's enormous mansion could compare to the houses that rested on Steve's street. She was not even sure the houses qualified as mansions; they were more like miniature towns. She tried not to gape at them and seem too fascinated. A couple seconds later, they pulled up to a gated entrance. Two large gates with the name "Sanders" engraved into them held the large estate that belonged to the Sanders family property. Next to the gate was a small booth with a man in it.

"Hey, Leonard," Steve greeted, "This is Kristin."

Kristin leaned forward to be visible and waved at the elderly man wearing a tailored suit.

"Afternoon, sir. Hello, Miss," he replied.

"Is my dad home, Leonard?" Steve asked the

nice old man.

He replied, "No, sir. He has a business meeting in New York, remember? He'll be back tonight for dinner." His tone was warm and respectful, yet comfortable. It was obvious he and Steve had known each other awhile.

"Ah, that's right. See you later, Leonard."

Leonard tipped his hat towards Steve and then pressed a button, which opened the gate. As they drove, Kristin tried to contain her excitement. She had never seen such an estate in real life, only in home magazines. There was a long, winding road that led up to the house. Green grass was everywhere, and Kristin admired all the beautiful flowers. Certainly, they had a hundred gardeners to maintain it all. Finally, the house was in view. In front of it were fountains in the shapes of swans. Bushes that spelled out the word "Sanders" surrounded them. Its design was that of a traditional mansion, and it was made completely of brick. Kristin gaped at the house. It was at least 20,000 square feet. Kristin suddenly realized why Eliza had probably been so into Steve. Eliza wanted to marry rich, and Steve definitely fit into that category.

Steve parked in the circular driveway and looked to Kristin. "Finally here," he said.

Kristin smiled at him, trying to maintain her composure. In a way, she was amazed. She swallowed hard and tried to imagine if the inside of the house could be even better than the outside. Indeed, it was. The house contained a movie theater, three pools (one of which was in Steve's room), a game room, a spa, a small tanning salon, and a kitchen larger that Kristin's entire first floor. The house had chandeliers made from diamonds hanging, and even paintings that Kristin swore she had seen in art museums. Despite the grandness of the house, it still felt homey. Kristin felt like it was a place full of memories. "Your house is gorgeous," she said. They were standing by the shiny, grand piano in his living room. She looked up at the high ceilings in admiration.

"My mom designed it all," Steve said and looked around as if it was his first time seeing everything, "It's too much for me, sometimes. I live in a house that's a big as some villages. It makes me feel bad, ya know?"

"You can't help it, Steve. You were born into this lifestyle," Kristin said.

"I know, but I'd rather we give some of that money to charities. Anyway, you want to go back to the kitchen? I can have George make us something delicious. That man is a god in the kitchen."

Steve was right, George was definitely a god in the kitchen. Steve and Kristin sat sitting at the kitchen table, both stuffing their faces with the four cheese lasagna he had whipped up. As Kristin ate, she thought about all the calories she was eating. She would definitely regret this in the morning. In the meantime, she took advantage of the moment. She and Steve had really bonded, and in that short amount of time, she began to forget about all the bad things that were happening in her life. Never in a million years did she imagine she would be in Steve Sanders' kitchen eating home cooked food made by his personal chef.

Steve began telling her about his family and his

life. He had an older sister in college, named Maggie. She was twenty-two years old and in medical school at UCLA. She could tell from the way he talked about her that he loved her. From his description of her and all the stories he told Kristin, Maggie was a smart, independent, and beautiful girl, everything Kristin strived for. And the fact that she went to UCLA was icing on the cake. Then, she found out he had a brother, Jack. Steve revealed that his brother was in the NFL, which Kristin was completely shocked to know. Why hadn't she heard that before? She usually knew everything; how had she missed that bit of information?

Steve noticed her facial expression when he said it. "I know, it's pretty cool, right? My brother is the coolest guy ever," he said.

"What's he like?" Kristin asked excitedly. She genuinely enjoyed learning more about Steve. He had such an interesting family, and every single one of them was perfect. One was a big-time lawyer, one was in med school, could it get any better?

"He's pretty nice. I miss him a lot, though. He and I used to be partners in crime. We used to tear this place up," he said while gesturing to his house.

Kristin smiled a bit. It was so cute seeing Steve talk about his siblings.

Steve explained that Jack was pretty preoccupied with his fiancée of two years, Sierra. Apparently, their big wedding was coming up, and Steve was being dragged to all sorts of tastings, fittings, and other pre-wedding activities. Between all that and his career, he barely had time to

Dodgeball Mystery

breathe, much less travel to Michigan.

"I know you wish you could have more time with him, but you only are engaged for a short amount of time. There's no better feeling than being in love," Kristin said.

Steve responded, "That's the thing. I know he's in love with her, but I don't know if he wants to marry her. He's only twenty-five."

"Have you talked to him?" Kristin asked.

"No. I don't want to offend him," Steve told her.

"Well, sometimes the truth hurts. Just be honest. He'll appreciate it, trust me," Kristin said. Kristin also learned a lot about Steve's mother. In a way, she reminded her of her own mother. From what Steve told her, she was strong and determined not to mention a great multi-tasker. Currently, she was in India doing charity work through her non-profit organization. As Steve told her about his mother's life, Kristin was amazed at how giving she was. Apparently, when she was not running her home garden, she was always doing work with her charity, visiting children's hospitals, or volunteering at soup kitchens and shelters. She seemed like the perfect human being. She managed to balance family and business— something Kristin hoped to do one day. It suddenly became clear to her why Steve was such a nice guy—he had had a proper upbringing. His parents had obviously taught him to be selfless and kind. Kristin suddenly wanted to become nicer too. Maybe she was about to experience some type of life-changing metamorphosis. "I really want to meet your mom," Kristin said to him. She could tell by the look on Steve's face that he was surprised.

"Really?"

Kristin nodded.

"I'm sure she would love to meet you as well."

Kristin was now surprised. She asked him, "Why do you say that?"

"Well, because you're a really nice girl. I think my mom would be happy to know that I've moved on to a girl that is actually good for me."

Hearing those words made Kristin's heart melt, but she was torn. She just did not think getting into a relationship with Steve was good idea. They had agreed to be friends, and that's the way she wanted to keep it, at least until her life got back to normal. Then again, Steve was an amazing guy. Kristin tried to wash away all her thoughts about his perfect hair, perfect eyes, heck–who was she kidding? Everything about him was perfect. Kristin tried to change the topic. "So, your mom likes to garden?" she asked.

"Loves it," he replied. "It's her favorite little hobby. We have a garden outside in the backyard. What about your mom?"

Kristin laughed and then said, "Nah she isn't into gardening." They both laughed. Kristin blushed a little.

He explained, "No, I meant what is she like?"

"Oh! Well, she's nice, she's funny. I guess she's just like most moms. She's really strong, too. She works a lot. I'm really proud of her, don't get me wrong, but sometimes I wish I had more time with her," Kristin admitted. She felt like she was spilling such personal details to Steve, and in a weird way it felt good to let some things out.

"I know how you feel," he said. Kristin watched

Steve play with the fork on his empty plate. They were both finished eating. "High school sucks; it'd be nice to have my parents around to help me out. It's not like I never see that; I just don't see them as much as I'd like. I get it, though. They've got to work for all of this." Steve gestured towards their surroundings.

"Tell me about it," Kristin said. She ran her hands through her hair just thinking about how stressful school was. "My mom is already talking to me about colleges and the ACT and the SAT, and all this other stuff. It's overwhelming."

Steve said, "I think sometimes they forget that we're just teenagers. And we want to have social lives."

Kristin nodded her head in agreement. She began thinking about her future and all the great things she wanted to accomplish. After going to NYU, she planned on becoming a broadcast journalist. One day, she knew she would have Matt Lauer's chair on the Today Show. She loved talking, so what job was better than being on TV and getting to tell people about what's going on in the world? She knew it would be hard to get to the top, but that didn't matter. In fact, she was looking forward to the journey on the way there. She knew she had passion, and she knew passion could get her far. NYU was her dream school. Besides being in the wonderland that some referred to as New York, the academics were good, too. And what better place was there to study journalism than in the city that never sleeps, right?

Kristin felt that everything was perfect in New York. Everyone was different and proud to be different. There were so many different types of people, and there was so much to do. It was her personal paradise. She had a couple of cousins there she liked to visit whenever she had the chance. She could not wait to move there and start her life on her own. She'd make all her own decisions–she'd stay up all night if she wanted, eat ice cream for breakfast (okay, maybe not). Anyway, things would be different there. She felt like New York was the place where everyone discovered themselves. It was clearly the best place for a teenage girl fresh out of private high school. Kristin wondered what Steve wanted to do with the rest of his life. "Steve," she asked, "Where do you want to go to college? What do you want to do?"

"Well," he started, "I don't really know yet. You know how I play football, right?"

Kristin nodded.

"Well, my dad really wants me to be in the NFL, just like my brother."

"And do you want to do that?" she asked him.

"I don't know. I like football–I'd just like it so much more if I didn't live it, breathe it, eat it, and sleep it. It's almost like a chore now."

"You're really good at football, but you shouldn't do it if you don't want to. It's not the same if your heart isn't in it. You know what I mean?"

He replied after a sigh, "Totally. Hey, I know this is off topic, but I have a question. You know how every year the football team throws the annual Halloween Party?"

Kristin nodded.

"It's kind of a rule that every team member has to bring a date. Would you be mine?" When Steve noticed that Kristin looked skeptical, he added, "As a friend, of course."

She smiled before telling him, "Sure, I'd like that."

"I know I've only known you for a day, but you're so cool and down to earth. I'm not used to being around a girl who is so normal."

Kristin melted hearing this. She liked Steve, she really did, but she had not dated since Josh. And everyone knew that did not end well. She was not ready to go back into the 'relationship world' yet. Josh had really hurt her. And even though she hated to admit it, she had not completely let go of him yet. "Aww! Thank you." Kristin blushed and put her hands over her face in embarrassment.

The two of them spent time talking about random things, from whether they preferred Coke or Pepsi to their favorite TV show. Kristin found that they had a lot of things in common. For one, they both were pretty picky about where they kept their things in their rooms. Steve explained that he was horrible at being organized and that his parents would sometimes fuss at him about it. Kristin related completely to this; her mother was constantly coming into her room, and seriously, it was the most annoying thing.

She explained, "She'll put everything away and organize it so much. I'll come in later and won't be able to find anything for days. When I was six, I'd come in my room not knowing that she'd organized everything and I'd start screaming and yelling, and I'd go around snatching things out of drawers trying to make it messy again."

Steve laughed after hearing this. For some reason, hearing Steve's laugh made Kristin laugh; his laugh was contagious. Steve said, "That's hilarious. I can only imagine what you were like when you little. What would your dad say when you did that?"

"He would just laugh and calm me down. He was good for that sort of thing," Kristin recalled smiling. She continued, "If he were alive today, my mom and I would definitely fight less. Don't get me wrong, I love her to death, but I guess you can say he was the peacemaker of the family."

"What do you fight about?"

"A lot of things. She picks a fight about every little thing. Once, I spent five grand shopping and she totally threw a fit!"

Steve's eyes bulged.

"What?" Kristin asked innocently, "There was a huge sale. What girl can resist a good sale?"

Steve simply laughed.

Kristin then regretted having said this. The last thing she wanted Steve to think was that shopping was the only thing she was good at doing. He was so well-rounded. He wasn't an obnoxious snob like some of the students at their school. He was extremely sweet. He told her that he loved little kids, something that Kristin could not relate to at all. The most experience she had with children was the rare occasion that she would have to babysit her younger niece for a few moments, while her aunt was in the bathroom. At first, she actually liked younger children. She had to admit that they were pretty darn cute. They just did not seem to like her. It was as if she was a child repeller.

Steve told her that his cousins were always coming over to spend time with him. Kristin could only imagine the trouble that a bunch of kids could cause around Steve's house. Then again, there was an insane game room, cabana, and theater. Kristin mentally shuddered at the thought of a bunch of little children running through his house causing mayhem. Kristin admired Steve for even being able to put up with all of that. She bet that he looked insanely adorable while chasing and playing with them. There was nothing more attractive than a guy who was good with kids, and watching things like that made Kristin's heart soften like butter.

"Your family sounds really great," Kristin said. She looked up, so that her eyes could meet Steve's.

There was a small pause.

Out of nowhere Steve asked, "Why don't you just let me be your date? I mean, since you're going to my date to the Halloween party, I might as well be yours to Lianna's thing." Steve looked into her eyes, making her nervous.

"Oh, so now you want to come?"

Steve seemed confused, and replied, "What do you mean? I'd love to go with a beautiful girl like you—as friends of course."

"Well, if you don't remember...when you dropped me off at my house, you said that you didn't want to come to the Lianna Gibson party because I can't trust people. You did not want anything to do with me. And, even though it's hard for me to say, I was really hurt when you said that. I'm used to fighting with people, and them reaching out to apologize."

"I'm really sorry about that, Kristin. In all honesty, I was frustrated that you were so upset. I was trying to comfort you, but you just shut me out. I guess I just got angry at Lianna for making you upset that I took it out on you. I was a real jerk. Let me make it up to you," he pleaded.

Kristin just looked at him.

"Please," he added.

"Fine, you can go," she said with a soft smile. "It should be fun, now that I'm not going by myself. I kind of planned asking you anyway, I just didn't know when I was going to ask you."

"Oh, that makes me feel nice. So, you kinda *wanted* me to go with you?"

"Kinda, but mostly I just didn't want to go alone. And on top of that, Eliza is going to super jealous when she finds out. Just imagine her face when she hears that I'm going to a celebrity's birthday party. Totally hilarious."

"Not everything is about Eliza. Forget about her."

Kristin nearly cringed hearing this. Forget about Eliza? *"Yeah, right. Never gonna happen,"* she thought. It was so hard to forget about her; she seemed to be everywhere. Kristin had tried so hard to dethrone Eliza, but so far she had had little success. Last year, even though she and Eliza were freshmen, they had gotten invited to the football team's Halloween party. Eliza had chosen to go to the party and hang out with Maddie, while Kristin wanted to make Elizabeth feel better since hadn't gotten invited, and had opted to go trick-or-treating with her. Trick-or-treating was fun, but she always imagined how cool it must have been for

Eliza to be there. Kristin, Eliza and Maddie were the only ninth graders allowed. While Kristin was trick-or- treating with Lizzie, she was constantly texting Eliza about what was happening at the party. Elizabeth kept asking who she was talking to, and Kristin had made some excuse. It would have hurt Elizabeth to know that even though Kristin said she would much rather go trick-or-treating, she was trying to find out what was going on at the party.

Kristin thought about the time when they were at Mrs. Rivard's door yelling trick-or-treat. Kristin's fingers were focused on her phone.

"Who are you texting, Kristin?" Elizabeth had questioned.

Kristin lied, "My mom. She keeps checking up on us, even though we're in ninth grade! Funny, huh?" Kristin's voice sounded convincing, and a stranger would have believed it, but Elizabeth knew Kristin wasn't texting her mother. Kristin would have never admitted that she actually texted her mother. Elizabeth would've never suspected it was Eliza, she figured Kristin just didn't want her in her business. The whole time that they were trick-or-treating, Kristin and Eliza were "LOL"ing. Eliza told her that a senior was checking her out, and had brought her a cookie on a napkin, with his number written on the napkin. Kristin was slightly jealous. She could be there having some guy hit on her but, usually when Kristin and Eliza were together, guys used Kristin to talk to Eliza. After reading the text about the guy with the napkin, Kristin had asked Eliza to ask Steve what he thought of Kristin; she had a slight crush on him, and Steve and Eliza were not together at the time. The next day Eliza said that she'd forgot, when really Eliza had been too busy flirting with Steve, and he had been trying to escape.

Kristin snapped out of her flashback hearing Steve calling her.

"Kristin!" He said repeatedly in a singsong type of way.

"Yes?" she asked.

"I said what are you wearing to the party?"

Kristin dramatically put her hands in her head. She still had not even begun to look for a dress and shoes. How could she have forgotten? She always checked Nordstrom's website every morning on the way to school. Everything that was happening had really thrown her schedule off.

"What's wrong?"

Kristin's head was still in her hands. A muffled, but loud groan escaped her lips and she mumbled, "I forgot to get a dress. I haven't even started looking. I am freaking out so much right now." When Steve gave her a look of utter confusion, she said it again, this time slowing her words. She tried her best to remain calm as she spoke. "I *said*, I forgot to get a dress. I haven't even starting looking. I am freaking out so much right now."

"Maybe you will just have to wear something you already have?" he suggested.

"Ugh," Kristin groaned. Wearing something she already had? What was her life coming too? Next thing she knew, she would be wearing something from last season. As much as she hated to admit it, Steve was right. The only option she had left was to wear something she already owned. Her phone began to ring. She looked at it and saw the word, **Mom** on the screen. She stared at the screen for awhile, too scared to answer. Steve nudged her to answer it. Kristin swallowed hard and answered it. "Hi," Kristin said softly into the phone.

Within seconds, she heard her mother screaming. She was so loud that Steve could make out every word that she was saying. Mrs. Gregory's voice was squeaky; whenever she was angry, it became extremely high pitched. "Kristin? Where are you? I came to pick you up, so I went to the office and they said that you hadn't shown up to any afternoon classes. Where are you?"

"I'm uh, at Steve's house."

Her mother said, "I'm coming to get you. Text me his address."

"But Mom– "

"No buts, text me the address now!"

Before Kristin could get out another word, the line went dead. Kristin's eyes awkwardly shifted to the ground. Of course her mother had to embarrass her in front of Steve. Kristin apologized to him multiple times, trying to lessen her embarrass-ment. Being the gentleman that he was, he told her that it was no problem. Everyone's parents embarrassed them sometimes, right? Kristin and Steve awkwardly waited together for Kristin's mother to arrive. Kristin wondered what her mother would say. She prayed to God that she would at least be nice to him. After all, he had basically saved her that day. He had been so kind to her, even *after* she treated him like last year's Sevens jeans. Besides helping her abort the chamber that some people called school, he had opened his home to her, given her food, and listened to her vent. He didn't judge her; he just listened. At the moment, he was probably her only friend. Everyone else simply could not be seen with her. Kristin was thankful for their newly developed friendship, but there was no doubt that she missed Elizabeth. She wondered what she was doing, if she was thinking of Kristin, if she was mad at Kristin. So many thoughts were going through Kristin's head. Would things ever be the same between she and Elizabeth? Had she lost one of the people in her life who knew her best? All over a little party? Kristin tried to wash all those thoughts away. For now, she was going to live in the present—or at least try to. She figured everything would fall into place eventually. It was pointless to stress out now.

Kristin and Steve stood near his front door and gazed out the window. Just then, Kristin saw her mother's car pull into the driveway. Her mother swung the car door open. *"Oh god,"* she thought. Her mother strutted towards the door. Kristin and Steve both looked at each other. Kristin braced herself. She closed her eyes and counted down. She could hear her mother's heels getting closer.

Three.

Click.

Two.

Clack.

One.

The doorbell rang. Steve gave her a small smile and tried to reassure her that it would all work out. He walked over to the door and opened it, with his smile still intact. "Hi, Mrs. Gregory," he said sweetly.

Her mother glanced him over quickly and then turned to see her daughter. Kristin rushed over to her mother and embraced her in a tight hug.

Her mother did not return the favor. "Please get off of me," she ordered. Kristin released her mother slowly and awkwardly stood looking at her. "Come on, Kristin. I can't believe you." The look of disappointment on her face crushed Kristin.

Steve said, "I'm so sorry, Mrs. Gregory. I never meant to upset you. It's just that Eliza was really mean to Kristin at lunch today. Kristin was crying, and I was just trying to help her out."

"Thank you for apologizing, young man. Kristin, let's go!" Her mother opened the door and started for the car.

"Bye Steve," Kristin mumbled. She and Steve quickly hugged.

"What about the party?" he asked.

"Text me later tonight about it. Thanks for everything, Steve. That was really nice." Kristin's mother was already at the car, while Kristin was still at the door.

Mrs. Gregory yelled for Kristin to come. Kristin waved good-bye to him and ran to catch up with her mother.

Kristin slammed her house door and threw herself onto her living room couch. The car ride to her house was possibly the most awkward experience she'd ever had. It was completely silent, except for when Kristin turned on the radio. She could have almost cut the tension with a knife. She wanted to explain herself to her mother, but she was so embarrassed about what'd happened.

"Kristin, come here," her mother called from the kitchen.

"Yes, Mom?" Kristin nervously paced around the large room.

"So, who is this Steve boy?"

"I already told you; he's just a boy from my school. I don't know how else to describe him."

"Do you at least know his last name?" her mother asked her. She folded her arms and gave Kristin the I'm so disappointed in you look.

Kristin wished she could say a magic spell that would make her mother disappear and forget that her daughter had ditched school with a boy she barely knew. "Sanders. Steve Sanders," she mumbled.

She saw her mother's eyebrows scrunch together. She could tell that Mrs. Gregory was mentally connecting the dots. It would only take about two seconds for her to put the pieces together. "That's funny, Michael Sanders has a son named Steve."

Kristin remained silent.

Mrs. Gregory studied her daughter's facial expression. "Wait, is he Michael Sanders' son?" Her mother asked with a smile.

Kristin sighed. She knew this would happen. Her mother was going to get all excited about the fact that Kristin and Steve were friends, and then she'd try to play matchmaker and get them together. All because Michael Sanders was the biggest lawyer in Michigan and her business role model. "Why didn't you tell me that?"

"Because it doesn't really matter to me, but it obviously matters to you."

"What does that mean?" her mother asked. She put her hand on her hip.

"Your whole mood just changed when I mentioned his dad. It just seems like you'll do anything to help boost your rep." After Kristin said that, she realized how ironic the statement was. Just a little while ago, she was the exact same way.

"Kristin, that's not true, but I'll let it slide because you seem to have had a rough day. Mind telling me what happened?"

Kristin explained to her mother everything that had happened in school. She told her all about the cafeteria incident, and the MyPage hate account. Kristin also mentioned to her mother that Eliza wanted Kristin to stay away from Steve. As she spilled all the beans, she felt a few tears in her eyes. Her mother reached over and wiped them away from her daughter's pretty face.

"Aww, honey, you must have been so embarrassed."

Kristin rolled her eyes. "No one would sit with me at lunch, everyone was whispering, and pointing, and laughing. Steve was nice enough to actually talk to me, and he suggested that I get away from all the drama at school."

Kristin's mother wrapped her arms around her daughter and gave her a tight hug. Her words came out a little muffled, "I can't believe that happened. Monday, I'm going up there, and I'm going to give Edwards a piece of my mind." She pulled away and looked Kristin in the eyes.

"No, Mom. That'll be embarrassing." Her mother gave her a look. "Please, Mommy." She batted her long lashes in the most innocent way possible.

Mrs. Gregory stated, "Fine, but if anything else happens, I'm going to be there." Silence filled the air, but not for long. "So, did you say that you're dating the son of Michael Sanders?"

"Okay, I'm going to my room now," Kristin said.

"Wait–I have something to tell you. Julie called and said that Elizabeth's party is definitely not happening. She'd like for all of her friends to come to the hospital tomorrow at one o clock. There's going to be a small celebration with cake and ice cream. Elizabeth's been miserable in that hospital, so she's looking forward to tomorrow."

"Mommy, I'm not going to see Lizzie. She's still probably mad at me."

"Well then you should call her or text her, or do that messaging thing you kids do, my My–whatever it's called. As a matter of fact, why don't you go do that now? If you do it, I'll let you go to Lianna's party tomorrow tonight."

"Mommy, please don't make– "

"Kristin!" her mother began. The tone of her voice said it all. Kristin knew that at this point it would be wise for her to just cave in. She slowly made her way upstairs.

Kristin paced around her room. She felt nervous, antsy. Her eyes glanced at the picture of Lizzie and herself at a Selena Gomez concert. The two girls looked as if they had just won the lottery. Selena was one of Kristin's favorite artists. The concert tickets had been a birthday gift from Elizabeth's mother. The cute picture made Kristin a little sad.

Her hands felt like clams. She had not felt this nervous since she tried out for cheer in 4th grade. As she walked around, she stopped at her desk, and turned on her laptop. She figured that the best way to contact Lizzie would be through MyPage messaging. As she signed into her MyPage account, she heard her cell phone ringing. *"Saved by the bell,"* she thought. Before she could say hello, the person on the other end spoke.

"I thought we had a clear understanding. You were supposed to leave Steve alone, remember?" Eliza spat.

Kristin wished that she had let it go to voicemail. She'd rather have an awkward conversation with Elizabeth than have to listen to Eliza's obnoxious voice. She decided it was time to give the little troll a taste of her own medicine.

"Listen, and listen good. It's not *my* fault that *you* couldn't be a good person and treat him nicely. You had to cheat on him. That's just you, Eliza. You always mess something up. Now, what else do you have to say because I have a comeback for everything! I'm sick of you, so you can shut up and go somewhere else with your crap. Eliza, I have a life and I have things to do. I don't have time to fight with you about stupid little things. I don't know, maybe you don't have real friends. Maybe you guys never hang out with each other outside of public, and that's why you have so much free time to bully people." Kristen paused a beat and continued. "Maybe you don't think you're pretty, and that's why you always call me ugly. Maybe, you don't really like yourself and that's why you hate me. Maybe you love being popular so much that you think everyone else is a loser. I don't know what it is but, what I do know is this: Eliza, you're the most horrible person on the Earth. I don't care how good your makeup looks or your hair or anything else. Underneath all of that, you're really ugly. None of your friends even like you. They all call you terrible things behind your back, and they snicker at you when you aren't looking. You think everyone likes you, but really they don't.

They just like everything you have and they use you. I feel bad for you. I really don't care what you do to me. Oh, and you can try to take Steve away if you want to. No matter what, he'll like me. Why don't you get it? We aren't friends anymore. You ignored me for a long time. You can keep bullying me if you want. Just know that Steve will be the shoulder I cry on." Kristin could hear the faintest of sniffles through the phone. Was Eliza actually crying? Kristin ignored it and continued, "One day the kids at school will stop following you, and you won't be able to control them."

Eliza replied while holding back tears, "I don't need to make people hate you. They already do. Just check your messages on MyPage, and you'll see." Eliza had hung up.

Kristin felt a sense of satisfaction. There had been a lot bottled up inside of Kristin. She wasn't the type of person who could hold in a lot of anger but, she'd managed to do it with Eliza, until today. The one thing Eliza was right about was the MyPage messages. Kristin's MyPage mailbox was filled with hate mail, and death threats. She felt sick when someone called her a "blood-sucking loser who's dad killed himself because he was sick of

her." Kristin then checked her email. She had one
email, and it was junk mail. It was from one of her
favorite stores. "What should I say to Elizabeth? I
could say hi, but that's too casual or, I can say hey,
but that's too friendly, and we're not really on good
terms," Kristin thought aloud. She decided to say
"how's it going?" After sending the text she stared
at her phone. Instantly, Elizabeth replied.

Lizzie - What do u want
Me - Just wanted to say hi
Lizzie - Don't
Me - ?
Lizzie - Eliza told me everything she said u
told every1 you didn't care about me
Me - It's not true I just thought YOU were
mad @ me!!!
Lizzie - Save it, have fun @ Lianna's don't
bother coming to the hospital
Me - I'm not even going to Lianna's party
Lizzie - Just leave me alone, kay?
Me - Fine, so we're not friends this is
stupid
Lizzie - We are NOT friends, get over it
Me - Okay, bye

Well, that was settled. Lizzie wanted nothing to
do with Kristin. Obviously, Eliza had been telling
Lizzie a bunch of lies. Kristin prayed that Lizzie
would realize Eliza was just being her
manipulative self. She could not imagine what it
would be like to have Lizzie and Eliza both plotting
against her. Lizzie knew all of her secrets. Would
she share those things with Eliza? Would Eliza use
the information as ammunition to make Kristin's
life even worse? Kristin pushed all her unanswered

questions out of her head. She decided to get a good night's rest and tackle everything the next day.

The next evening, Kristin lay on her bed while reading a celebrity gossip magazine. Three gossip magazines later, Kristin went to the kitchen and grabbed a pint of coffee ice cream. She carried it to her room, tablespoon in hand. As she shoved the ice cream into her mouth, she messaged Maya on MyPage. No answer. She tried messaging the rest of her friends. Again, no answer. She then messaged a random girl who she recognized from her school. No answer. None of her friends were answering. Next, she checked to see if anyone new had requested her to be their friend. Nope, in fact, ten people had blocked her. She saw that Steve was online. Kristin messaged him a simple 'hi'. Her phone started ringing. "Lucky you, you've got Kristin Gregory live!" Kristin joked.

She heard Steve's rich laugh through the phone. "Hey, Kristin? So, can I pick you up at eight for the party?" he asked.

Kristin's eyes bulged. She dropped the spoon that was in her hand. She had completely forgotten about the party. Kristin replied with a mouthful of ice cream, "Oh, yeah, sure." She put the ice cream on her night table and stood up. In one hand, she held the phone and in the other she took her hand out of its messy bun.

"So, was your mom upset?"

"A little. I'd love to talk, but I have to go get ready."

"It's six o' clock," Steve exclaimed.

"I know, I know but, you know what they say, it's never too early to get ready."

"They say that?"

"They do now. See you soon, Steve." Kristin ended the phone call and rushed to go take a shower. As Kristin stood in her bathroom, wearing a silk robe, she applied makeup. She hadn't done her hair yet. It was six o' clock in the evening, and she was doing her makeup precisely. She had to admit that makeup was one of her specialties. Her mother was great at it and had shown her all her tricks. Before doing her makeup, she had gone to the nail salon up the street from her for a manicure and pedicure. A smooth french tip coated her perfectly trimmed nails. Her mother was friends with the owner, so of course they managed to fit her in. As she applied blush, she admired her classic french-tip nails.

It was now 7:00 p.m. Kristin had straightened her hair, done her makeup, and whitened her already white teeth. She meandered through the cocktail attire section of her closet. Her eyes landed on a pink fit and flare dress that her mother bought for her over the summer. There were perfectly-sized cutouts on the side of the midriff. She settled on nude pumps with a bow on the peep-toe part. The pumps were made especially for Kristin by an Italian designer, so no one else would have them. Oddly enough, she felt relieved that she never got the chance to go shopping. Her outfit was perfect. Even though she and Steve had sworn to only be friends, she hoped that he thought she looked pretty.

She was sitting on her bed bored and anxious. She had decided not to put on her dress until seven-forty-five, because if it had any wrinkles in it whatsoever, she simply would not be able to wear it. Just then her phone buzzed. She ran to the bathroom to get it. Steve had texted her saying that he was on his way. Kristin replied, "ok." She was so excited and couldn't wait for the party! As she jumped up and down, she singsong, "I'm going to Lianna Gibson's party! I'm going to Lianna Gibson's party! Oh my gosh! Oh my gosh!" After calming a bit, which took about five minutes, she carefully slipped on her dress, trying not to put a single wrinkle in it.

She put on the luxurious shoes. The moment reminded her of Josh, her ex-boyfriend. He'd always surprise her with random gifts like that, but to be honest, Kristin never cared about the materialistic things he gave her. They were just a bonus. She loved him. Josh was amazing. He had perfect, dark brown hair, bright hazel eyes, teeth that were a little crooked, but cute and perfect in a weird way. Josh made her smile, laugh, and even cry sometimes with his sweet charm. They'd been dating each other for one year when Kristin walked into the gym and saw Josh standing there kissing a girl with platinum blonde hair.

Kristen immediately recognized the girl as Tisha McDonald. Tisha was that girl in school who tried to steal everyone's boyfriend. She was all over every guy. Kristin had run out of the gym silently, and went into the bathroom and cried. She instantly snatched off the charm bracelet Josh had given her for her birthday. The gold bracelet was beautiful, but Kristin hated him now, so she hated it too. She thought about flushing it, but decided that idea wasn't good payback. She wrote a note to him saying 'we're over' and taped the bracelet to it. When Josh found it in his locker, he raced to find Kristin. When he finally found her, he was a little out of breath. "Kristin, what's this about?" he asked with the note and his bracelet in his hand.

"What do you think it's about?"

"Why are we breaking up? I love you. You mean everything to me."

"Really? because I think Tisha thinks you love her." Josh's face fell.

"Tisha is just my friend. You've got it all wrong! Please just listen to me, bab-"

Kristin turned her face as a tear fell. "Don't you dare call me that, you pig! Just save it! What a downgrade. Anyone named Tisha is not girlfriend material," she said while looking away.

"I don't know what you are talking about."

"Stop lying, Josh. I saw you! I don't care what you have to say. Okay? By the way, I'm returning everything you gave me. Bye."

Kristin slipped on her shoes, grabbed her phone and clutch, and went downstairs.

Chapter 4
A Night Out

"Hi," she greeted Steve. He was outside at her door and looked amazed. He couldn't keep his eyes off of the dress. "You look beautiful."

"Thank you. You look nice, too."

Steve kindly put her arm in his and escorted her to his car. He opened the door for her. Kristin felt like a real princess. She had not felt that way since Josh. Thank God she had met Steve. He was a real gentleman.

Kristin and Steve were in line to get into the party. They'd walked the small, red carpet already, which was fun. Kristin felt like a superstar in front of all of the cameras. Steve had seemed a little tense as they were posing. *"He's probably just nervous,"* Kristin thought. They were getting close to the entrance of Lianna's beautiful mansion. Two girls stood in front of them with tight mini dresses on.

Kristin overheard the brunette say, "That guy behind us is so cute!"

Her blonde friend replied, "Yeah, but he's with

that girl."

It didn't seem like Steve was paying attention to anything that was going on. The blonde slightly turned around, and then turned back. Kristin rolled her eyes. What wimps. They were too afraid to simply say hello to a boy. Then again, if she saw a guy like Steve with a girl like herself, she would be afraid too. Kristin could not have been happier when it was finally the two girls' turns to be admitted into the party.

The tall security guard said, "Okay, you two enjoy the party." For some odd reason, the brunette lingered behind. Kristin figured the girl probably was planning talking to Steve. Kristin could hear the music blasting from inside of Lianna's mansion. "Name, please?" he asked Kristin.

"Kristin Gregory. Party of two. He's with me."

The security guard searched the list, and went through all of the papers. "Miss, you're not on the list."

"Check again," Kristin said confidently.

She watched him flip through the papers over and over. "You're not on the list. There's nothing I can do, Miss."

The brunette girl piped up, "Is there a way that I can get them in?"

"No, ma'am. You only have a party of three under your name. Now, if only one of them wanted to get in, that would be fine."

"Kristin, you can go. I'll wait in the car," Steve offered.

"No. I came here with you."

The security guard butted in, "You better decide who's going to go quickly!"

Kristin said, "Steve, that girl has been checking you out this entire time. Tonight would be perfect for you guys to talk, and dance, and have fun. So, you go. Don't object. I'll call a cab or something. Go and have fun. I'm sure there will be other chances for me to meet Lianna."

"Well, how do I know that you'll make it home safely?"

"I'll text you when I'm in the cab. Don't worry, Steve."

Steve continued, "You're the one who loves Lianna Gibson, not me."

"Yeah, but you're the one with a hot girl waiting on you. So, go, tomorrow you can tell me all about the party. And make sure you take lots of pictures for me."

Steve quickly hugged Kristin. "Thanks, Kristin, you're the best."

Chapter 5
An Awkward Run-In

Kristin watched Steve walk off with the girl. She grabbed his hand, and they continued walking in the house. She sighed, and started walking away. Why did she feel a little sad? She'd already told Steve that she wanted to be friends, but it still seemed like he liked her. And now, he was holding hands with someone else. Kristin pulled out her cell phone; she figured now was a good time to call a car service. As soon as she started dialing, her phone died. *"Great,"* she muttered. *"I guess I'll walk,"* she thought. Kristin started down the sidewalk. She knew her way home from this area. How hard could it be? Twenty minutes later, she was still walking. She got a little bored, and started humming. Her feet were really hurting. She was even so bored that she started talking to herself. "I can't even believe this happened. At least Steve is having fun." A white sports car started driving down the street. It started going extremely slow. *"Oh no, someone's going to kidnap me!"* Kristin thought. She'd seen this thing happen a million times on all those criminal mysteries she watched. She tried not to look in the direction of the car. It continued to follow her for maybe a block, when the driver rolled down its window.

"Hey Kristin," the person called. Kristin looked over and saw Josh in the car.

"What do you want, Josh?" she asked rudely. It was hard enough seeing him at school, and now she had to see him outside of school.

"Need a ride?" he yelled.

"No, I don't need a ride!" she snapped even louder.

"I'm not letting you walk home from here. It'll take you hours. And you have on heels too. Get in, now or I'm coming over there," he said calmly.

Kristin decided it'd be easier to just get in the car. She huffed and got in and buckled her seatbelt. She stared at the road ahead, but could see him looking at her out the corner of her eye. "Why are you looking at me?" she finally asked.

"Because you haven't said a word. Spill. What happened, and who are you jealous of?"

"How do you know I'm jealous of someone?" Kristin asked suspiciously. She folded her arms and turned to face Josh.

Josh smiled and said, "I think you forget that I used to be your boyfriend. I know you, Kristin. Whatever guy just broke your heart was stupid."

"Well that's where you're wrong. He did not break my heart," Kristin insisted.

"So, something did happen with a guy?" Josh asked.

"I'm not talking about it—especially with you."

Josh asked, "Why not?"

"You know why: I hate you," she stated casually.

Josh looked horrified. "I get it," he admitted, "But that doesn't mean I'm not still in love with you."

Hearing those words shocked Kristin. She suspected Josh still had feelings for her, but she was not expecting him to suddenly pour his heart out to her. As much as she hated to admit it, hearing him say that made her feel weird.

She replied, "Cry me a river, Josh. You're a cheater. You take advantage of girls."

Josh didn't respond; he just shook his head. He pulled into a gas station. Josh opened up his glove compartment, and got his wallet out. Kristin spotted the charm bracelet she'd given him back when they'd broken up in the glove compartment.

"Why do you still have that?" she asked Josh while staring at the bracelet.

Josh said quietly, "It means something to me." He was staring at the steering wheel. Finally, he exited the car.

While Josh was inside of the gas station, Kristin looked through his glove compartment. If he had kept that stupid bracelet, who knows what else he had. She looked at the bracelet, causing memories to come rushing back. She thought of all of the fun times her and Josh had together. There was go-cart racing, laser tag, dining, spontaneous walks, talking on the phone for hours, and just hanging out. He, Kristin and Elizabeth had all become friends. They'd have the best times together. She had loved him; he was her first real love. In her head, she'd always thought that they would be together forever but, he'd ruined it all. When she put the bracelet back, she noticed love notes and poems that she'd given him. She saw the watch she'd given him for Christmas. She could not believe that he had kept all of that stuff. There were lots of cards that they'd given each other too. Kristin had returned every single card he'd given back to him...and he'd kept them. Wow. She saw him coming out of the store. He pumped the gas and got back into the car.

"Josh," Kristin started, "Why do you still have all the stuff from when we were together?"

He seemed a little shocked. Kristin could tell he didn't know what to say. "Because those things remind me of you. Of *us.*"

"Yeah, but I don't even like you anymore. I dumped you because you cheated on me, remember?"

"Kristin, I'm not trying to argue, I don't want to argue right now. I've had a really long night and it seems like you have too, so can we just please not annoy each other right now? I would really love this car ride to be peaceful, wouldn't you?" He asked politely.

"Absolutely."

The rest of the car ride to Kristin's house was silent. The only thing playing was the radio. The air was very tense and awkward. It was a little funny to Kristin how bad of a liar Josh was. Did he really expect her to think that he cared about her? Why would she think that for a minute? She knew that he was a good liar. After she'd broken up with him, Josh had kept saying that there was nothing going on between him and that girl. Kristin wouldn't buy it just for a second. A kiss means a little more than 'nothing.'

Josh pulled into Kristin's driveway. They both were just sitting there in the car. Josh was the first one to break the silence. "Just so you know, I think Eliza was really wrong for humiliating you like that at lunch." Kristin didn't say anything. He continued, "We all know how much of a jerk she is. Good thing Steve left the table to comfort you. And, I don't think that you were the one who threw the dodgeball at Lizzie either. I'll be the first one to tell Edwards that, okay?"

"I don't need you to talk to Edwards. I can handle my own problems, Josh," she said meanly.

"Why are you so defensive? You hate any and everything I say. Even if I say something really nice to you, you're still rude to me. I don't understand," he said. Neither of them was looking at each other.

Kristin was staring out the window about to get out of the car. "Yeah, and I don't get how you could cheat on me, and then lie about it. I'm the one who had my heart broken. And last time I checked, girls weren't over-friendly to their ex-boyfriends who cheated on them! So sorry if I can't be all smiley towards you." A few moments passed. "Thanks for the ride."

"No problem," Josh muttered.

Kristin slammed the car door and walked up onto her porch. She was inside the house when her doorbell rang.

Kristin opened it, and saw Josh there. "Look, don't yell at me. Just hear me out, okay?"

Kristin nodded and put one hand on her hip.

"I'm so sorry for everything, Kristin. I loved you, I'll always love you. And, there was nothing going on between me and Tisha that day in the gym. She kissed me! I don't even like her. I never did. Whether you believe it or not is your choice but I'm sorry. And whatever jerk hurt your feelings tonight was stupid for doing that, because you are the most beautiful girl I have ever met on the inside and out. I miss you. I miss us hanging out together, I miss our friendship. I know that you are mad at me. I understand why. I wouldn't want to be friends with someone who I thought cheated on me either. And I'm not asking you to be friends with me or get back together with me. Just forgive me. Please."

Kristin looked Josh in the eyes. He was waiting on her to say something. She replied, "No one hurt my feelings today, for your information."

"Oh. It just seemed like…you look gorgeous, and you're wearing a beautiful dress and heels. Your hair is done; obviously you were going somewhere today. And it just looked like you were sad. I'm not trying to be in your business. Anyway, do you forgive me?" Josh looked so vulnerable and sincere.

Kristin couldn't help but feel bad for being mad at him. "Why would I need to forgive you if you insist that you didn't cheat on me?" Kristin questioned suspiciously.

"I'm sorry for the whole thing. I'm sorry that we had to end things the way we did. I'm just sorry."

Just then Josh's phone rang. "Hi," he said to the person on the other end. Kristin looked at the ground. Josh was still standing on her porch. "Yeah, I'm at a friend's house right now," Josh said into the phone. A few more seconds went by, and then Josh said, "It's okay. I get it. I'll see you next month. Bye."

"Who was that?" asked Kristin.

"That was my mom. Apparently, she's going to be out of the country *another* month. So, I'm at home by myself for *another* whole month. I swear, I never even see her." There was anger in Josh's voice. Kristin already knew the situation between Josh and his mother. His mother was a major businesswoman, and she was barely ever home. His father had not been in his life for awhile. She'd leave him with a credit card for a month or so, and he could buy whatever he needed.

"Oh, are you hungry?" Kristin asked hesitantly. She didn't want him to come in but she knew he'd be lonely by himself at home.

"Yeah, I'll probably stop for something on the way home. I should go."

"Josh, if you want to, you could just come in. I have some leftovers. I know that you're probably sick of fast food," Kristin said.

Josh responded, "Are you sure?"

"Just come in, J, before I change my mind," Kristin said with a half smile. He smiled back and entered her house. It had been a long time since she had called Josh by the nickname she'd given him: J. Obviously, he was just as happy to hear it as she was to say it; she could have sworn that his eyes sparkled when she said it.

Kristin and Josh sat at Kristin's dining room table. She watched him devour the spaghetti that was on his plate. She felt bad for him. She knew what it was like to have a parent always be working. Unfortunately, in Josh's case, his mother was practically never home. Things had been that way ever since Kristin could remember. Josh's nanny, Pippa, had raised him and his little sister. About a year before Kristin and Josh broke up, Pippa had decided to return to her home country of Italy. Apparently, her childhood love had recently proposed the idea of them getting married and living in Italy. Josh was heartbroken, as was his little sister. Pippa was the mother they never had. When Pippa left, Josh and his sister had no one. There was no point in looking for another nanny. No one could ever replace Pippa. The only adults Josh was ever around at home were the housekeepers.

For a split second, Kristin thought of asking Josh to stay awhile. They could watch movies, play board games, and make ice cream sundaes just like old times. They were both lonely, and she figured Josh would have fun. Then, she remembered the pain he had caused her. The idea vanished just as quickly as it had come. She suddenly felt a painful sensation in her feet. She looked down at the stilettos she was wearing. She must have been so distracted by how annoyed she was with Josh that she never realized how badly her feet hurt. Kristin slipped off her heels and threw them. Josh looked up from his plate and turned his head to where the shoes had landed.

"Feet hurt?" Josh asked.

Kristin nodded.

"So, you were at a party?"

"Yeah." Kristin didn't want to be rude, but she wasn't in the mood to talk, especially not with Josh.

She had invited him in to eat to be nice, not to have conversation.

"What kind of a jerk would let a beautiful girl like you walk home by herself?"

Kristin rolled her brown eyes. "He's actually not a bad guy. And thank you."

"For what?"

She said shyly, "Calling me beautiful." She tucked a strand of her pin straight hair behind her ear and looked down at her nails. She looked up. Her eyes locked with Josh's.

"It's the truth," he said quietly. A few moments passed. "So, you're going to tell me the story on how you ended up walking home by yourself?"

"No, it's embarrassing."

"Aww, come on. Don't act like you've never told me something embarrassing. Remember when you told me that you were still afraid of the dark?" Josh asked while smiling.

Kristin looked down. "Yeah, how can I forget? You laughed every time you saw me for two weeks." Kristin and Josh both laughed for what seemed like forever.

"Those were the days," Josh said. More silence. "So, what were you looking forward to at the party?" Josh inquired.

"Dancing with him," she replied. She soon realized that she'd said the word "him" and mentally kicked herself.

"Oh. Kristin has a crush," Josh teased.

Kristin rolled her eyes and smiled. "I do not have a crush. He's a friend. I just was looking forward to dancing. Trust me. I barely even know him."

"Who is he? Who's my competition?"

"None of your business and you don't have any; you and I will never be a thing." Kristin's voice raised a little. She saw Josh smile a little. "What's so funny?"

"Nothing, you're just cute when you get mad. Your eyebrows scrunch together and your voice gets all high-pitched. And your eyes get a little darker."

Kristin said, "Shut up!"

"You know, I haven't met someone great since you," Josh said to her. I can't find a girl who loves me for me, and not because I'm a popular jock who's friends with Eliza Parker, and is on the football team. It sucks."

"I'm sorry," she said while staring into his eyes. As annoying as he could be, she could not deny that his eyes were like little pools of hazel perfection. She wasn't interested in a friendship, especially after their horrible breakup. She just wanted to make him feel better.

"Yeah, me too. Thanks for the food. By the way, Allison misses you," he said referring to his five-year-old little sister. Allison and Kristin had been extremely close when Josh and Kristin dated. She would take her to the mall, the movies, Chuck E. Cheese, and other things like that.

"I miss her too."

"Well, I better get going. Have a good night," he replied. He flashed his charming smile.

"Thanks for the ride," she replied just as nicely. As Josh backed out of her driveway, she let out a loud breath. She was so confused. Was it possible that tonight was the start to a friendship with Josh? Hopefully, not. And why did she feel mad at

Steve? Why was she a little envious about the fact that he was at Lianna Gibson's party and she wasn't? Kristin decided to forget about it until the morning. Her mother had left her a voicemail. Apparently, she was spending the night at Carol's because she was too tired to drive home. Carol was her co-worker and best friend. Now, Kristin was stuck, something she hated being. If Elizabeth wasn't in a hospital and they were on speaking terms, she probably would have come over to Kristin's house and slept over. Kristin sat on her bed thinking. She really was starting to miss Elizabeth. Maybe she should call Elizabeth, swallow her pride and apologize. Maybe. Kristin decided she would sleep on it.

The next morning Kristin woke up around 9:30 a.m. She walked to her mother's room. Mrs. Gregory was sitting in bed with a laptop on her lap, and her BlackBerry next to her.

"I see you're home," Kristin said from the doorway.

Her mother looked up at her through her glasses. Even first thing in the morning with no makeup on, Kristin's mother managed to look flawless. Kristin walked over to the bed and sat down next to her mother. She rested her head on her mother's shoulder and watched as she typed away on the computer. One of the things she admired most about Mrs. Gregory was her work ethic. Kristin knew that her mother worked so hard because she wanted to give Kristin a better life than she ever had. Mrs. Gregory finally finished whatever she was working on and shut her laptop.

The two spent a couple of hours watching their movies. They were halfway through *The Notebook* when Kristin's phone began buzzing. It was Steve. She didn't want to be rude and take a call while they were spending quality time together, so she texted him.

Kristin - Hey. You called?

Steve - Yeah. I wanted to know if you were available to hang out today. My place?

Kristin - Sure :) what time?

Steve - About an hour

Kristin - Sounds good. See you then

Kristin looked up at her mother, who was focusing intently on the movie. "Um, Mom?"

"Yes, Darling?" Her mother's eyes were still on the screen.

"Would you mind if I left our movie session? My friend invited me over to hang out, and we both know I'm pretty low on friends right now, so..."

"No, of course not, go be with your *friend*." Mrs. Gregory put extra emphasis on the word, friend and wiggled her eyebrows in a flirtatious manner as she said it. Kristin rolled her eyes and lightly hit her mother's shoulder. "That reminds me, how was the party last night? Did you and Steve have a good time?" Another eyebrow wiggle.

Kristin jumped off the bed. "I'm going to get ready. Love you Mom," Kristin said as she ran out of the room. After showering and doing her daily routine, Kristin stood in her closet. Since when was picking an outfit so difficult? "Ugh," she groaned as she tried to maneuver through all of the clothes. No matter how many times she went shopping, she still felt like she had no clothes. She sifted through her jeans, and found a pair of plum colored skinny jeans. Perfect for the autumn weather. They still had the price tag on them and everything. Kristin decided to pair them with a black silk button down blouse, which she immediately recognized as being Elizabeth's. She decided on brown riding boots to top the outfit off and neatly pulled her silky hair into a high ponytail. Perfect. She heard her phone buzz again. She walked over to her nightstand and was surprised to see that Josh had texted her. Apparently, he just wanted to thank her for being kind to him the previous night. Her encounter with Josh had not only been extremely awkward, but also a bit depressing. Not only did she secretly miss him as a boyfriend, she missed hanging out with him. He had been one of her best friends and it was hard to let go of him, but Kristin knew it was the right thing to do. When they were sitting at her dinner table the night before, she wanted to tell Josh, "I miss you. Let's just start over as friends." She tried to block all thoughts of Josh out of her head; it was just making her confused and even worse: stressed. Kristin attempted to be happy and get excited for her day with Steve. It would be nice to just have fun for the day. One of the pros to hanging out with Steve instead of Josh was that she did not feel the need to have her guard up with Steve. In her heart, she felt that Steve would never hurt her the way Josh did. Kristin knew that once school started back up on Monday, her life would go back to sucking. She had no friends at school, she might get expelled, and her best friend was in the hospital. *"Oh well,"* Kristin thought. At least she was getting a chance to spend some time with Steve.

Chapter 6
Maybe This Won't Work

Kristin carefully pulled her car around the curves of the road leading to Steve's house. Driving definitely was not one of her strong suits; she had just gotten her license a few months back. Even she was surprised to find out that she passed. The road test had been a tad disastrous. It probably didn't hurt that her mother knew a couple of people down at the DMV. She pulled up to the gates of his home, and Leonard opened them for her. After parking her car and checking her reflection in her front mirror, she rang the doorbell. Without seconds, the door opened.

"Hey," Steve said. He was wearing sweatpants and a white t-shirt. Still, he managed to look good. He always looked that way; relaxed yet effortlessly good-looking. "You look so fancy," He said.

He closed the door, and Kristin took off her shoes. She didn't want to take any chances on scuffing the beautiful floors. They looked particularly shiny that day, that she could practically see her reflection. "How was I supposed to dress?" she wondered.

"More comfy. It's okay, though. You look really pretty."

Kristin's cheeks flushed a bit. She tried biting the inside of your cheek to keep from smiling, but that didn't work. She couldn't help but to smile. Steve was so kind to her, always complimenting her. When he said it, he sounded so genuine, and maybe even a little too good to be true. He suddenly stumbled on his words. "Not to say that you don't look pretty when you're not dressed up. Ya know, 'cause...I meant, it's just that."

Kristin said while laughing at his cuteness, "I know what you mean." There was an awkward silence. Kristin looked off in the distance pretending to be distracted by a lamp that she spotted. Finally, Steve broke the silence and suggested that they go look for snacks and then watch a movie.

Kristin followed his lead to the kitchen. The pair rummaged through the pantry and picked out their favorite junk foods. Kristin carried a package of Twizzlers in her hand, while Steve carried a box of chocolate chip cookies, marshmallows, and a can of Pringles. Minutes later, Kristin was still inside the pantry. Steve, on the other hand, was gathering some cans of pop from his refrigerator and had already selected all his snacks of choice. Kristin stood motionless inside the pantry. She was faced with the ultimate decision: She didn't know whether to get a bag of party mix or Doritos. A quick game of "Eenie Meenie Minie Mo" settled that. She reached for the Doritos bag and picked it up. Behind it was a box of vanilla frosting.

Suddenly, she had the perfect idea. She grabbed the frosting with her empty hand and walked to where Steve was standing.

He looked up and gave her a weird look. "I'm not trying to be rude or anything, but are you really going to eat plain frosting? I mean, I guess I could get you a spoon or something," he said.

"I have an idea," she announced proudly.

"To eat frosting," he concluded. Kristin shook her head. "So your idea is to not eat frosting?"

"No, silly. My idea is that we should make cupcakes," she explained.

Suddenly, Steve made the "Oh" face. "It'll be fun, I promise. Do you have stuff to make them?"

"Yeah, probably. Here, I'll get the recipe book and tell you what ingredients we need." Steve walked over to one of his cupboards. Steve pulled a thick, weathered-looking book down from a shelf. She watched as he flipped carefully through the tattered pages. Kristin figured the old book must have been a family recipe book. After all, the thing looked older than Kristin's great-grandmother. It must have been passed down through tons of generations. Something about the book made Kristin smile. A few seconds passed. Steve finally stopped turning the pages. "Here we are," he said, "Classic vanilla cupcakes with butter cream frosting."

Kristin's stomach nearly grumbled at the sound of such deliciousness. Steve read the list of ingredients necessary, while Kristin searched and found them in the kitchen. She placed them on the kitchen island. Gathered was butter, sugar, flour, eggs, vanilla extract, whipping cream, and a foreign ingredient that Kristin had never heard of–confectioners' sugar. After everything was out, Kristin looked at Steve. Her heart melted when she realized that he was probably only making the cupcakes to make her happy. She was ripped out of her thoughts by the sound of Steve's voice. "Huh?" she asked.

"I said we should probably get the electric mixer. You gotta stop daydreaming so much," he said. He playfully elbowed her. Her cheeks flushed red, and she looked up at him.

"Oh, sorry. I was just thinking but anyway, yeah we probably should get the mixer," she said.

Steve nodded and went to one of the cabinets to retrieve it. He sat it down on the island carefully. Just like the recipe book, it looked like it had weathered a storm. Or two. "This," he said while plugging in into an outlet was my grandmother's. My mom swears this mixer has magical powers. Baking is kind of a big deal in my family."

"So you know how to make the cupcakes?" Kristin asked with a smile. Steve burst out laughing. "I'm guessing that's a no?"

Steve nodded. "What about you?" he asked.

Kristin shook her head no. "Well this should be interesting." Kristin held the bowl down while Steve used the mixer. Kristin had to admit that she was having a good time. She had never really baked cupcakes before either, so she was happy to finally learn. They had already put all the ingredients for the batter into the mixer. As he mixed, a bit of flour got on Kristin's nose. Kristin seemed to be so into holding the bowl that she did not even realize it. Steve noticed and started laughing. Kristin made a confused facial expression. Steve stopped the mixer and explained what he was laughing at.

Kristin made a straight face that said Are you kidding? which only made Steve laugh harder. He wiped the food off of her face and decided it'd be a good idea to get even. She gasped and pointed behind Steve's head. "Oh my god, what is that?" she asked in the most worried tone she could muster. Instantly, he turned around to see what she was talking about. While he was looking, she got a small handful of flour out of the bag.

Steve said before turning around, "I don't see what you're talking..." Before he could finish his sentence, Kristin threw the bit of flour onto his face.

Instantly, she started laughing uncontrollably. This time, Steve was the one with the straight face. Kristin put her hand over her mouth in effort to control her laughter, but she just could not help herself. Steve pretended to be upset, but it was hard for Kristin to take him seriously with all the flour that was on his face.

"Oh you think this is funny?" he asked.

Kristin said while laughing, "Hilarious."

Before Kristin could recognize what was happening, Steve grabbed some flour and threw it at her. She returned the favor and practically covered him in flour. Soon, they were in a full-fledged flour fight. They ran around Steve's kitchen laughing and drowning themselves in the ingredient. Kristin had not laughed that hard in a very long time. For a moment, she forgot about all her problems and felt like she did not have a care in the world. She could tell by the look in Steve's eyes that he was also enjoying it. She chased him around the kitchen island. There was so much flour on the floor that they ended up falling to the floor. They both lay on the floor laughing their butts off. Needless to say, the cupcakes turned out to be delicious.

After baking and eating cupcakes, Steve and Kristin watched his favorite movie, *Taken*, in his theatre. During the movie, Steve put his arm around Kristin. She tried to ignore the butterflies she felt in her stomach. She couldn't understand why she was feeling this way. This was not supposed to happen. They were supposed to be just friends. She was not supposed to like him. Kristin couldn't figure out what was wrong with herself. Kristin Gregory did not fall for guys within a couple of days. Her affection had to be yearned for and worked for. She tried her best to focus on the movie. Steve comforted her during the scary parts. It reminded her of Josh. He always held her whenever she was afraid. Oh, goodness. Did she really just compare Steve to Josh? What was life coming to? Before she knew it, the film credits were on the screen.

"Did you like it?" Steve asked her, as the lights came back on.

Kristin nodded her head and stretched.

"Let's go eat. Is pizza good?"

"Pizza is perfect," Kristin said.

Kristin and Steve sat in his kitchen eating the pizza. While Kristin's brain was thinking about how delicious it was, Steve's head was in a totally different place. He couldn't help but think about how much he had begun to like Kristin. She was smart, funny, and pretty. Plus, she didn't seem too phased about the fact that he was insanely rich. She seemed real but he knew that she didn't want to be his girlfriend. His mind then wandered back to the girl from Lianna's party who had gotten him in. She was beautiful, no doubt about it. They'd exchanged numbers and even talked earlier that morning. He'd even asked her out on a date. Now, sitting here with Kristin, he felt guilty. Was it rude of him to ask that girl out when he had just told Kristin how much he liked her? And was he starting to actually like the girl from the party too?

Kristin brought him out of his thoughts. "How was Lianna's party? I know it must have been amazing. Did you talk to that girl?" she asked while pulling a strand of her straight hair behind her ear.

He said, "Yeah, I did. I actually got her number."

Kristin nearly choked on her pizza. She did her best to look happy for him.

He asked her, "Are you mad?"

"No, I'm happy for you. Why would I be angry? We're just friends, anyway." In Kristin's head though, she was quite confused because just yesterday Steve was telling her how much he liked her. He sure moved on quickly.

"Just checking. Actually, Julie and I have a date tonight. Around seven. Maybe you could help me plan it?"

Kristin was surprised when he said this. He wanted her to help him plan his date with some other girl? "Sure. Well, you have the greenhouse outside."

"Oh yeah? And we have the Mary Garden!"

"The what garden?" Kristin asked with a confused look.

"It was named after my great-grandmother Mary. It's this huge garden filled with tons of flowers. It's really pretty. She'd like that, huh?"

"She'd love it," Kristin replied quietly. She felt a weird pang of jealousy. "You and her could go on a walk through the gardens that would lead to an intimate dinner set up in the middle of it. You could have pretty lights set up and everything. It'll be nice," she said imagining the scenario.

"That's a really good idea. Thank you so much."

Suddenly, Steve's phone began ringing.

Kristin glanced at the screen subconsciously. She recognized the number, but couldn't quite pin whose it was. Suddenly, she knew exactly who it was.

"Hey, man?" Steve exclaimed into the phone. He put it on speaker. Suddenly, she heard his voice. How had she not realized that Josh and Steve were friends? After all, they were on the same football team.

"Hey? What's up, bro?"

"Nothing much. Just hanging out with Kristin."

"Kristin? As in Kristin Gregory?"

Kristin looked down, gulping slowly.

"Yeah. Are you guys friends?" Steve looked over at Kristin.

Josh replied through the phone, "Nah, she's my ex! Dude, you're trying to date her? Man, that is so against the bro code!"

This caused Steve to raise an eyebrow at Kristin.

Kristin felt the tension in the room rising faster than her heart rate during the Nordstrom Anniversary Sale.

"I didn't know," Steve exclaimed while glaring at Kristin. How could she not tell him?"

"Yeah. I was at her house last night."

"You were what?" Steve exclaimed.

Josh went into detail, "I found her walking down the street by herself last night from a party. The date she was supposed to go to the party with turned out to be a prick. She was really upset. I ended up eating dinner at her place. It was fun, actually. Tell her I said hey."

"Yeah, I will," Steve replied while looking at Kristin blankly.

Kristin sank in her chair.

"Josh, I gotta go," Steve said into the phone.

"All right. Hit me up later, though."

"Okay. Bye."

"Bye."

Kristin looked everywhere but into Steve's eyes. She felt embarrassed. Now, he knew. He knew that Josh and Kristin were once a 'thing.' Kristin knew that she would have to tell him eventually, but she did not want it to be now. She knew the question was coming.

"Why didn't you tell me that you and Josh dated?"

"You never asked?" she said, but it came out more like a question.

"That's not the point. You didn't even mention to me that you knew him. He and I are on the same football team!"

131

"I didn't think it was important. He's my ex. We have no interest in each other now, anyway."

"Then why was he at your house last night? I asked you what you did last night and you said you watched a movie. You failed to mention that you had dinner with Josh. You really thought I wouldn't find out?"

Kristin stood up, taking her plate to the sink. She turned around. "Why do you care in the first place?"

"Because you lied and you told him I was a prick!"

"I never said those words. I never even intended on him taking me home. He just...happened to be there."

"Did you kiss him?" Steve asked simply.

Kristin shrieked. "Eww! No. Josh and I are not even like that anymore."

"Why did you lie in the first place?"

"Because I didn't want you to think there was anything between Josh and me. Honestly, I don't understand why you're so upset. You and I are just friends. Besides, you have Julie anyway."

"Oh, so you were trying to make me jealous?"

Kristin replied, "No!"

"Then why did he sound so protective of you?"

"I don't know. We were very close, and he seemed to have a bit of a hard time with the breakup, as did I. Truth is, I still care about him. A lot but, I'm not in love with him. Can we just not talk about this?"

"Why do I feel like you have a wall up with me?" Steve paused, "It's like you don't trust anyone because you had a bad experience with him.

Everyone else has to pay for what he did."

Kristin felt her hands clench. *"I don't know, maybe it's because we just met,"* she thought. Had he really just insulted her like that? Sure, Steve had been very nice to her so far, and treated her like a princess but he didn't know her. She said instinctively, "Maybe I should just go."

He said quickly, "No, don't. I'm sorry."

"No, it's okay. You've got a date to plan. Good luck tonight."

"Thanks. You sure you're okay?" he wondered.

"Positive. I'll see myself out. Don't worry."

"Bye."

She waved good-bye before turning around to walk away. "See you at school Monday."

Chapter 7
I Miss You

Hours later, Kristin sat on her bed thinking about the day's events. She wished so badly that her father could come back. Right now, she could really use his advice. Surely, he would have some wise words for her. Most likely, he would tell her not to worry about Elizabeth, and that she would eventually come around. He would hold her in his arms and tell her that not to worry, that everything would be all right, that he loved her. His advice on the Josh situation would probably be to forgive him and to move on. Even though he had never met Josh, she had always thought they would have been the best of friends. And of course, her father would believe her about the dodgeball incident. His death had been so sudden; she'd never really had time to fully grieve. As soon as he'd passed, she and her mother had to find a way to plan the funeral quickly. After that, they were preoccupied with getting all his finances settled, which was tiring. Truthfully, Kristin had never really sat down and cried it out. She knew that crying would not take away the pain. Nothing could. Ever. She'd lost him, and he was never coming back but that didn't mean that Kristin had to silently suffer forever. Kristin knew, as well as her mother, that all the material things they'd bought after her mother got that new job were just a way for them to try and forget about his death, and for a little while, it had worked.

As she curled up into a ball on her bed, she started to cry. Tears endlessly flowed. A feeling of hopelessness washed over her. She felt like everything in her life was screwed up. Kristin needed to talk to someone who would understand, and with her mother not at the house and Lizzie mad at her, the only person left was Josh. Sniffling, Kristin wiped her eyes. She picked up her phone and dialed his number.

"Hey," he said groggily.

"It's Kristin." She hoped that her voice did not give away the fact that she'd been crying.

Josh replied before chuckling, "I know. I have caller ID."

Kristin laughed nervously. Talking to Josh was scary, even though she had just done it the other day. He still had that effect on her; Josh could still make her stomach flutter.

"You okay? You don't sound too good."

"I'm not," she paused and took a breath, "That's kind of why I called you."

"How about I pick you up from your house? Does that sound okay?"

"Yes." She sniffled once more.

"All right. See you soon."

"**Thanks** for picking me up," Kristin told Josh from the inside of his car.

"No problem."

Kristin glanced around his car. In the backseat, she noticed his varsity jacket. Her mind flashed back to the night when he'd taken her to homecoming. Everything about that day had been magical, from the time she woke up to when she fell asleep while thinking about how amazing Josh was.

"You have to wear this," Josh said sweetly while placing his varsity jacket on her. It was a tradition at their school for the girlfriends of the guys on the team to wear their varsity jackets to homecoming. "I know it covers up your beautiful dress, but·" "I don't care. I'm proud to be wearing it." She gave him a smile. Kristin and Josh slowly leaned into each other, until their lips danced shyly. Both of them could feel the eyes of Josh's and Kristin's mother's eyes on them, but they couldn't care less. Kristin wrapped her arms around his neck, while his fit perfectly around her small waist. They were standing by the staircase in her house, with both their families there to take pictures of the cute couple. Josh's grandparents, aunts and uncles, little sister, and his mother were there. Kristin's grandparents and her mother had come as well.

"You are so special," he whispered. "You're my number one girl. I just want you to know that." A big smile soon spread across his handsome face.

"And you're my number one guy," she whispered back.

"Um, we're still in the room," Josh's mother said at that point.

"Mom," Josh exclaimed.

Kristin laughed. She leaned into his ear, "We kiss all the time. Don't be pouty."

"Kristin, you are so pretty!" His mother, Karen, told her. Kristin was shocked that his mother had even been able to make it. She'd been so busy. Josh had begged her to come.

Kristin gracefully replied, "Thank you. I didn't know if this dress was too much. I mean, I thought it might be too short and stuff." Kristin was wearing a black, fit and flare dress. It stopped a little above mid thigh.

"Everything is perfect," his grandfather added.

"Okay, you two need to take pictures together." Kristin's mother had her hands clasped together, along with a huge grin. Obviously, she was happy.

"Absolutely," agreed Josh's mother.

His grandmother said proudly, "You too are just adorable together! You remind me of me and George," she said, referring to Josh's grandpa George. Kristin looked at Josh. As crazy as the thought was, she definitely could picture being that old with Josh one day. Everyone began laughing and talking amongst themselves.

"Guys, we need to take pictures! The homecoming starts in an hour," Josh said quickly.

Kristin said to him, "Josh, it's okay. Our families just want to "savor the moment." Don't act like you don't love the attention." She pinched his cheeks. He scrunched his nose up.

"I know, I know. I'm just ready to go spend time

with you at the dance. You know, have a good time?"

"We are going to have a good time. I promise, but for now, let's spend time with our families."

"I think it's about time we take pictures," Josh's father said loudly.

Everyone gathered around Kristin and Josh and snapped pictures. Flashes came for what felt like a decade. Josh's arm was wrapped around Kristin's waist. They took a few pictures of them hugging, as well as one of them putting their boutonnieres and corsages on each other. Finally, it was time for them to leave.

"Have fun you two. Be safe." Kristin's mother shouted to them as they pulled out of Kristin's driveway.

"You excited for tonight?" He asked while they drove.

"I'm nervous. I know that for sure."

"Don't be. Everything will be perfect!"

When they arrived at the dance, Kristin held his hand tightly as they walked to the entrance doors of the school. As they were just about to walk through, Josh stopped and said, "Wait. There's something I need to tell you."

"Okay," she said calmly. Nothing could prepare her for what he was about to say next.

"You're amazing. I'm really happy that you are my date tonight, and I'm even happier to call you my girlfriend. You're special. I love talking to you, getting to know you even more, going on dates...I love everything about you. Homecoming is going to be perfect. I was so nervous when I saw you tonight. You look amazingly beautiful. Your hair is

perfect, that dress is so pretty. You just look perfect, Kris. I hope you know that I realize how lucky I am to have such a supportive, smart, beautiful girl like you in my life. You had your guard up at first, but I helped to bring it down. I know you took a big risk by letting me in, but now that I have your heart now, I am never going to let it go. I'm going to work hard to make every day you spend with me better than the last. I know this sounds crazy since we've only been going out for 3 months, but what I'm trying to say is that I love you."

Kristin's breath hitched. "J-j-josh. I love you too."

As Kristin sat in the passenger seat of the car, she suddenly felt a little uncomfortable. Here she was, in the car of her ex-boyfriend, for the second day in a row. Josh seemed perfectly normal. She would have never imagined she would even be able to stand being in the same room as him. Obviously, Josh didn't at all feel weird about being around Kristin.

"So, um, you mind telling me what you were doing at Steve Sanders' house earlier?"

"We were just hanging out and having fun until he got all weird and jealous. And honestly, I kind of understand where he's coming from, but I feel like it was also kind of stupid, ya know?" Kristin was reluctant to tell Josh everything that happened. Then again, she had no one else to vent to at the moment. And despite everything they had gone through, she still trusted him with her secrets.

"So he was jealous of me?" Josh asked.

Kristin could sense a strange sense of satisfaction in Josh's voice. "When you mentioned that you were at my house yesterday, he got really jealous. It didn't help when you told him that I called him a prick, which I didn't."

"So Steve was your date to the party?"

Kristin nodded slowly. This situation was getting more and more awkward. Not only did Josh used to be her boyfriend, he used to be one of her best friends, but now it was like they were strangers. Except for the fact that she knew that no matter how much she had tried to act like she hated him, there was a part of her that always wanted him to be her best friend again. Kristin sighed in slight frustration. She watched Josh's facial expressions. He pressed his lips together. He was obviously frustrated too. One of the things she had learned about him was that he pressed his lips together whenever he was trying to find the right words to say. That was another thing about Josh. He always put so much effort into giving advice. It was like he thought every single word out carefully. He always did give the best advice.

"Look, Kristin, just give him time to cool off, okay? He was jealous and to be honest, I would be too if I was him. You're an amazing, beautiful girl. You and I were hanging out *alone* together, and I'm your ex. It does sound fishy. Even you have to admit that."

Kristin let Josh's words set in for a bit. He had a point. "Okay," she said, "Maybe you are right about that, but he's the one who has a date with that girl at the party. Just the other day he was so into me. Now I just feel like it was all fake. Is that wrong of me?"

"No, it's not. Kristin, I think you are over thinking this. Don't. If you feel a certain way about him, don't try to fight it. Relax and let fate take control."

After a few minutes of driving, Kristin realized how tired she was. She found herself quickly dozing off. Josh's words replayed over and over again in her head. "Let fate take control." Josh was right. She was definitely over thinking things with Steve, as well as things with Josh. Instead of getting angry at Steve, she should have been more understanding. She decided she was going to just go with the flow. Still, she was a little confused. She had felt immense butterflies when she was with Steve, but she was not completely sure how she felt about him yet. She figured it would all become clear if it was meant to be.

Kristin was sleeping softly when all of a sudden, she heard Josh's voice say quietly, "Wake up. We're here."

She fluttered her eyes slowly and looked around. They were at a burger place, of course. Josh loved burgers. Josh got out of the car first and opened the door for her. They walked into the restaurant. It was relatively small. The chairs were old and wooden, but the food was delicious. It was a favorite of everyone. Kristin and Josh sat in a booth facing each other. There was a light right above them, illuminating both of their eyes. Kristin avoided eye contact and kept looking at the menu. Josh was the first to break the silence.

"Why were you crying earlier today on the

phone?" Josh asked her. Right after he got the words out, a perky waitress approached their table. They both ordered the same thing: a bacon cheeseburger with no onions and extra pickles. The waitress wrote down their orders and walked away.

"She was nice. Sometimes those waitresses can be so rude," Kristin said.

Josh said sternly, "Do not change the subject. Why were you crying? Come on, you know you can tell me anything." He looked straight into her eyes.

"I was just thinking about my dad and how he'd be able to help me through everything that's happening. Elizabeth is not talking to me at all, Steve hates me now, and I'm here talking to *you* about it all."

"You miss him," Josh stated simply. When they were dating, Kristin talked about her father a little, here and there but only the positive things. She never once brought up his death or that she missed him.

"Yeah." She looked up at him and into his eyes. "I try to cover it up by spending all that money and buying stupid, material things, but that doesn't work."

"That's because you're not the girl who acts all superficial and materialistic or stuck up, for that matter. You try to be perfect, but truthfully you're perfect when you act like yourself. I understand that you're always trying to outshine Eliza, but that's not always important. Think about it like this: Is anyone of this high school popularity stuff going to matter in ten years? No. We'll all be living our lives and doing more important things than hosting parties and competing for attention. This stuff is so temporary. Focus on the permanent things that matter–family, relationships, friends. I know it can be hard. Trust me, I get caught up in all of it too sometimes."

Kristin suddenly felt more relaxed. Josh understood Kristin, unlike Steve. He knew why she tried so hard to beat Eliza, instead of telling her not to try like Steve had. "I'm trying to get better at that. Ya know, just focusing more on the important stuff. And not everyone agrees with you about my true personality being perfect. Half the people who I call friends would not stand by me if I didn't shop at Neiman Marcus and you know that. Heck, the other day when Eliza embarrassed me in the cafeteria, no one was there for me. The only person who comforted me was Steve."

"Kristin, I would have comforted you if– "

"If what? If your football friends had not been in the same room? Yeah, I know."

"That's not true. It's just that I doubt you would have accepted any type of comforting from me at that time. You know I'm here for you. You can hate me all you want, but you're always gonna be my baby."

"I *don't* hate you."

"Well, we didn't come here to talk about me. We came to talk about you."

Kristin agreed, "Exactly."

"So, are you nervous to go back to school?"

She tensed up. School had been on her mind a lot. Hearing Josh ask her that question made her realize that she only had one more day of hiding. After that, she would have to face her fears. All of them. "How'd you know that? Yes, I am extremely nervous to go back. Everyone hates me, literally! I could potentially be expelled, and even worse...have to go to...I don't even want to say the two words."

"Public school," he said for her.

"Thank you for not making me say it. I'm just really stressed out, and until now I haven't really talked it out."

"You can't talk to Steve?"

"Not like I can talk to you," she admitted honestly.

He saw the sincerity in her eyes. She missed him like he missed her too. "Gosh, I missed you," he told her.

She smiled and said, "I missed you too."

Chapter 8
Give Me a Chance

Kristin entered the school quickly. She was trying to look confident and not show how she was truly feeling. She'd put a lot of effort into the outfit she was wearing. A good outfit always helps, right? If she was going to be ignored by all her friends, she might as well look good while doing it. She was wearing a white, ruffled blouse tucked into a short, leather skirt. She had black high heels on her feet with her hair curled into perfectly cute, loose curls. As she marched to her locker, she fiddled with her fingers and cracked her knuckles–something she always did when she was nervous.

"Miss Gregory," a sharp voice said.

Kristin gasped. For some reason, the person's voice scared her. She jumped a little out of shock and then turned around. "Hi, Principal Edwards," Kristin greeted him, while crossing her arms.

"Come to my office, please.

"Um, I have Bio in...," she paused to look at her glossy watch that lay on her arm, "...Two minutes, and we're having a test so–"

"I'll write you a pass. Come with me."

Kristin sat with her arms folded in a chair across from Principal Edwards at his desk. Her lips were pursed together in frustration and she was tapping her foot. Any ounce of patience she had was slipping away more and more as every second passed. She looked around his office. Finally, her eyes landed back on Principal Edwards, who looked like he could use a spa trip. His crow's feet were so bad that it was disturbing her.

Principal Edwards finally spoke up, "Elizabeth's mother is not happy that her daughter is in the hospital because of some foolish child's irresponsible decision to try and knock out Elizabeth. She wants whoever did this to be put out of the school immediately. I have good reason to believe that you were responsible for Elizabeth's accident. I cannot continue to vouch for you."

"What evidence do you have? Elizabeth being in the hospital is breaking my heart. I love her; she's like a sister. I love her entire family. Of course I didn't do it! Yes, we may have been in a fight, but I could never hurt her like that. Please, Mr. Edwards. I know I have been rude to you, but I am so sorry. You have to believe me."

"Kristin, at this point there is nothing I can do."

"Let me guess, a few people who are out to get me came to you and told you that they saw me do it? Don't believe them. They just want to see me fall, which cannot happen. If I was able to prove my innocence, would you let me stay here?"

"Well, I guess," he replied slowly. What was Kristin up to? Whatever it was, Principal Edwards did not think it would be good.

"Okay. Give me 'till tomorrow to prove myself or at least figure out a way to do that. Please?"

He clasped his hands together and leaned forward on his desk. Kristin could see all the ugly, fine wrinkles in his face. He had crow's feet by his eyes. "Fine, but you've only got until the end of the day."

"Thank you, thank you so much! I won't disappoint you, Principle Edwards, I promise." Kristin jumped out her seat and began jumping up and down in excitement. She clasped her hands together happily. After a few seconds she regained her composure, gracefully smiled, and excited his office with the biggest smile on her face.

Chapter 9
A Plan is Needed

Kristin sat in English class without anyone sitting next to her. Apparently, no one wanted to sit next to her. She could not focus on what Mrs. Jacobson was saying; she was too busy thinking about how she could get anyone other than Steve and Josh to vouch for her innocence. She certainly did not have the support of Eliza or her annoying crew. Proving her innocence could only be done with the help of others, and at the moment the only person who she was completely sure would be there for her was Josh. Kristin would practically need the support of the entire school to show Principle Edwards that she had not thrown the ball. And, the only way to prove that she hadn't thrown the ball was to find out who had. How could Kristin do that in one day? As she sat deep in thought, she faintly heard someone calling her name, but she was too busy daydreaming about how great it would be if she could discover the person who was out to get Elizabeth and herself.

"Kristin? Kristin?" The voice repeated over and over again.

Kristin snapped out of her thoughts. "Huh?" Mrs. Jacobson said, "I have been calling you for the past two minutes."

Kristin looked around the room. She saw Eliza sending her a smirk. Eliza snickered while whispering something to one of her sidekicks. As she whispered into the girl's ear, she kept her cold eyes locked on Kristin. "I'm sorry, Mrs. Jacobson," Kristin sincerely said.

"Apologies mean nothing if actions do not replicate them, Miss Gregory," her teacher scolded in a preaching tone.

Kristin mentally rolled her eyes.

Eliza took the chance to add her two cents. "Mrs. Jacobson, don't be too hard on Kristin. Her entire life is crumbling before her eyes. She's going through some tough times."

Kristin looked away, feeling her temper flare up. She wanted to fire off at Eliza, but Mrs. Jacobson said hurriedly, "Eliza, please! Kristin, can you please answer the question."

"What question?" Kristin asked.

"I was asking you a question about the lesson that I just taught. Are you actually here or is it just your physical body?"

"Could you repeat the question?"

"Miss Gregory, you better buckle down. Whatever you have your mind on is not more important than getting a good grade on the English quiz tomorrow."

Chapter 10
You're Back

As she walked through the lunch line, Kristin scanned the lunchroom for Josh. As she went through all the tables of people, she saw Eliza's table. When she looked at Eliza's table, her eyes fell upon the back of someone. She recognized the person instantly. She nearly dropped her tray. Kristin felt her hands get all clammy. She rubbed them on her leather skirt, which only made matters worse. Suddenly, her body was stiffened and was incapable of movement. She realized she had been staring at the person when Eliza looked up, probably feeling a set of eyes on her. Eliza nudged the mystery person's arm and gestured in Kristin's direction. They turned around. Kristin's intuition was right; it was Elizabeth. Obviously, she was back in school. Did she know about Kristin possibly getting expelled? She had to have known.

Elizabeth's eyes locked on Kristin. Unlike usual, her eyes were filled with hate. She glared at her, and then smirked slightly. Kristin's face was motionless. Kristin quickly looked away, and Elizabeth turned back around. Kristin secretly looked at Eliza's table again. Why was Elizabeth sitting with Eliza and her friends? Didn't she know that Eliza was evil? Kristin's stomach felt queasy. That was happening a lot lately.

"You okay?"

Kristin turned around to find Josh standing behind her. He was wearing a football sweatshirt and khaki pants. "No. Get me out of here," she proclaimed quickly.

"Okay, let's go." He grabbed her wrist and dragged her out of the lunchroom and into the hall.

"I just can't believe Elizabeth returned to school and didn't even think to tell me," Kristin ranted. Josh was sitting there, politely listening. He was so good at those sort of things.

"You guys aren't friends. What can you expect?"

"No, we are friends. We're best friends. Best friends fight, and they claw at each other and push each other's buttons. They say mean things and get nasty. Best friends say they hate each other but, they always love each other. And they always make up!"

"You watch way too many movies, Kris."

"I have good news, by the way. I was planning to tell you the news before I found out that my best friend had betrayed me. By the way, shouldn't you be with your football friends?"

"Stop worrying. What's the news?"

"Edwards was going to suspend me, but I was able to get him to make a deal with me. If I can find prove my innocence by tomorrow or figure out a way to, I won't be expelled."

"That's great! How are you going to do that?"

"I don't know. Will you help me?"

He replied, "Of course."

Kristin suddenly felt bad for being so mean to him at first when he found her walking down the street after the Lianna Gibson party. "Josh, I'm sorry. I haven't exactly been nice to you, and you have been so kind to me. You listened to me...I never even explained to you the other day why I suddenly wanted anything to do with you. And you never asked either. I would have expected you to. I mean, we had a nasty break-up because you cheated."

"I did not cheat on purpose, but I'll let it go. I never asked because I didn't need to. You were weak, and as a friend I'm supposed to be here for you, even if you don't consider me a friend. Any bitterness I had towards you went out the window when you called me and I heard you crying, and not to mention trying to cover it up."

"Thank you for helping me. Friends?"

"Friends."

"I have a plan." Kristin said excitedly out of nowhere.

"What?" Josh asked.

"We'll have a trial. The entire school can be the jury. I'll get to tell my story, defend myself. I'll get a chance to prove that I didn't do it. Whoever wants to be against me can try to prove their point too! And then at the end, the school will vote either for or against me. If the majority of them vote for me, I stay and I'm not guilty. If it goes the other way, well..."

"It won't. Don't worry. We'll present the idea to Edwards tomorrow."

"This just might work."

Chapter 11
Nice Seeing You...Not

At the end of the day, Kristin could not have been more happy to leave the school. The school day had gone by more slowly than her hot yoga class that she occasionally took. All through her classes, she could not focus. People were constantly looking at her–staring at her. Finally, Kristin understood what it was like to be an outsider. Sure, she had never been as popular as Eliza, even when she was friends with her, but she usually had people around her at all times. Half the "friends" who she used to hang with were not even true friends. They were just following her because they could not be their own person. Before she and Elizabeth had their big blowout at Kristin's house, they had been becoming slightly distant. Kristin had been trying desperately to claw to the top of the social chain, even if that meant ignoring the few people in her life who truly loved her. She and Elizabeth had had a small fight a couple months before their huge one. Kristin had told Elizabeth that she could not accompany her on a trip to the movies one night because Kristin's stomach was feeling weird and she was too exhausted.

As Elizabeth was leaving out of the Palladium theatre in downtown Birmingham, Michigan, she spotted a familiar pair of Chanel Two-Tone Riding boots strutting down the street. "Kristin?" she called out, recognizing her. Kristin was walking side by side with Mackenzie Danvers, who was one of Eliza's minions. What was Kristin doing out? And even more importantly, why was she with one of Eliza's friends? When Kristin did not turn around after Elizabeth called her, Elizabeth ran to catch up with her. Kristin, however, had heard Elizabeth clearly. Of course she recognized her best friend's voice but she could not let Mackenzie think that. She and Mackenzie were in deep conversation about Ralph Lauren's latest collection and a new restaurant that had opened up in town.

"I heard they serve crepes," Kristin said excitedly.

Mackenzie strictly replied, "It'd take an entire Pilates session to burn off one, itty bitty crepe."

"Of course it would. I love Pilates. I love exercising period."

"You do?" Mackenzie raised an eyebrow.

"Yes! Maybe we should take a class together, and we could get some froyo afterward? That would be fun!"

"What about your friend Elizabeth? No offense, but she is not as fabulous as you are."

Kristin stammered, "Well, no I guess not, huh? She's really nice though. I've known her since forever."

"And I've known Weird Wendy from school since forever too, but that does not mean I'd ever be caught dead hanging out with her. If you and I are going to be hanging out, Elizabeth cannot be in attendance. Got it?"

How could Kristin make a decision like that so quickly? It was practically impossible. "Um...well..."

"I'll give you a couple of days to think about it. No worries"

"Okay," Kristin replied gracefully.

"You aren't that bad. I don't know why Eliza hates you so much. She'd flip if she found out that we were together."

"Yeah, I think..."

Suddenly, Elizabeth started shouting Kristin's name. She was about a foot away from Kristin and Mackenzie. Mackenzie whipped her long, dark hair, and turned around to face Elizabeth. Elizabeth scrunched up her nose when she caught a whiff of Mackenzie's perfume.

"Elizabeth, what are you doing here?" Kristin asked nervously.

Elizabeth folded her arms sassily, "I just finished seeing a movie. What are you doing here? You told me you were feeling sick."

"I-I-I..."

"Cat got your tongue? Save it."

Mackenzie said meanly, "Maybe Kristin doesn't want to be friends with you anymore."

"Is that true, Kristin?" Elizabeth looked a little doubtful.

"No, of course not, Lizzie." Kristin looked down at her peach colored nails. What was she thinking?

If she was going to hang out with Eliza's minions in order to possibly take over her clique, she should at least be smart enough to do it in a place where Elizabeth wouldn't be lurking.

"Oh, really? That explains perfectly why you blew off our movie outing," Elizabeth said.

"I didn't blow it off. I was feeling sick. Then all of a sudden my stomach felt better. I guess Tums really do work. And honestly, I wanted to surprise you by coming to the movie with you, but I figured since it had already started I'd be intruding. So, I called up Mackenzie to go shopping with me."

"Well, I don't believe you," Elizabeth said. "I'm leaving."

Eventually, Kristin and Elizabeth had made up. Sadly, their most recent fight did not have the same results. Kristin put her heavy school books into her backpack. She had a ton of homework to catch up on due to her "skip day" on Friday. Josh walked up to her locker, looking distraught.

"You look happy," she joked to lighten the mood.

"Yeah, right. I'm so screwed. Coach is on my butt. I wanted to skip practice today to help you work on your plan, but he told me that if I miss one more practice, I'm off the team."

"Josh, I'm not more important than your dreams. You know what I just realized? Both you and Steve love football and want to go pro."

"And that's another thing. Steve skipped the other day, and he had no consequences," Josh said angrily.

Kristin laughed a bit. "About that...Steve missed practice because of me."

157

"What?"

"He took me back to his place. We had pizza and made cupcakes. He was trying to cheer me up."

Josh scoffed. Kristin could sense that he was jealous of Steve, and Steve was jealous of him. She figured it was normal for him to feel that way towards Steve; after all, he had confessed his undying love for her.

"Don't be mad. We're just friends."

"You sure? 'Cause guys don't do all that romantic crap for nothing. They sure don't do it for "friends" especially the female ones. Trust me, I know these things."

Kristin's ears suddenly perked up. "You've been dating?"

Josh admitted, "I've been attempting it. It's not going well, though. No one ever seems to replace you."

"Josh, if this is your way of trying to win me back, it's not working. You and I can never be what we once were. And I certainly do not have time for this right now. I have a best friend to win back and a reputation to save. I thought we were moving forward–as friends. Gosh, you are just like Steve, always trying to rush things."

"I am not just like Steve. You know me much better than you know Steve."

Kristin took a quick gasp for air. She had never been in this sort of situation. Both Steve and Josh liked her, but both of them had also done things that disproved their claim. Josh had broken her heart, and Steve had asked out a random girl from Lianna Gibson's party. She certainly did not have time for "love" at this point in her life. Of course she adored being in love. It was a wonderful feeling, caring and loving someone else more than you do yourself...putting their feelings above your own just to make them happy. Love was amazing, but sadly it never lasted–at least as far as Kristin was concerned. It was a temporary joy. And who would want to risk everything for something temporary?

"I'm sorry, Kristin. I'll back off. We're just friends. Now, let's focus on our trial plan. Oh, here comes Eliza."

Kristin turned sharply. She saw Elizabeth walking with Eliza. What was this? Middle school all over again!

"Hello, Kristin," Eliza said smoothly.

"Elizabeth, are you okay? Oh my god, I missed you so much. I know I've been such a horrible person to you." Kristin embraced Elizabeth tightly.

Elizabeth did not return the gesture. She simply stood there while Kristin wrapped her arms around her.

Elizabeth quickly pushed Kristin off of her. "Will you stop hugging me?" she snapped.

"Why?"

"We are not friends anymore. Eliza told me what you did to me. She says that you wanted to get rid of me so that I would be out of the way."

Kristin found herself trying to think of words to say. "Elizabeth, you cannot believe that. You and I both know that Eliza is a conniving, evil witch. That's an understatement, actually, just think of all she put us through. Why would I want you out of the way? It makes no sense!"

"It makes perfect sense," Elizabeth said. Was it

possible that Eliza had brainwashed her that quickly?

"Well, it does not make sense to me. Explain it, please. I'm completely lost," Kristin replied.

"With me around, it was hard for you to improve your social status. I'm a "loser", correct? So you thought the only way for you to become popular was to not have anyone who weighed you down. And, for some crazy reason, you thought the only way to do that was to kill me."

Kristin chuckled. "I'm sorry for laughing but that sounds a little dramatic even for you, Lizzie. It's not only crazy–it's untrue. I'm genuinely worried about you, Elizabeth."

"Which explains why you never even called me during my hospital stay," Elizabeth said.

Eliza pipped, "If you're genuinely worried, you will leave her alone. I'm protecting her now. Now shut up and go away! Enjoy your short time at this school. You won't be here for long. And if you do somehow escape the wrath of Principal Edwards, I will swallow you up myself." She took a step closer to Kristin, so that they were only a few inches apart. "And then," she said, "I will chew you up and spit you out like the trash you are."

"Eliza, that's enough," Josh defended Kristin.

"And what are you doing here? Didn't you cheat on her last year? Not that I'm sticking up for her. It was probably in your best interest that you left her. Why don't you give me a call when you aren't busy?" Eliza winked.

Josh shuddered at the thought. "I *don't* like you, Eliza."

"Why are you back with Kristin? Josh, you're

popular. Always have been. You can do so much better."

"Let's get out of here, Kristin," Josh told her with a smile. He ignored Eliza's comment.

"I'd love to. But, first, Elizabeth can we talk?" Kristin glared at Eliza. "Alone, please."

Kristin grabbed Elizabeth by the wrist and dragged her over to a corner. She wanted so badly to get down on her knees and beg for forgiveness. Tears welled up in her eyes. "Lizzie, you have to believe me. I would *never* do that to you. You are my sister. Eliza is only trying to tear us apart. She's out to get me."

"It is not all about you."

"And what are you wearing, Elizabeth? You're dressed in designer wear from head to toe. You're morphing into a different person. Elizabeth, stop pretending to be someone you are not."

Elizabeth protested, "Why? It's okay when you do it, isn't it? And, I am not pretending to be someone I am not! Now, if you'd excuse me, I have somewhere to go."

"Stop running from me. Where could you possibly have to go? The school day is over. Elizabeth, I need your help–desperately. Edwards is threatening to expel me."

"If you're just dying to know, the girls and I are going out to get some lunch. And yes, I know about your possible expulsion."

Kristin laughed out loud. "The "girls"? Who even are you? I'm starting to think I never even knew you."

"I've got to go. See you around"

Chapter 12
I'm Not Okay

Kristin and Josh were sitting in her room creating a way for Kristin to market their mock trial idea to Principal Edwards. Kristin had waited for him after school in the stands until his football practice was over, and then he drove them to her place. She watched both him and Steve and she had to admit that Josh was better. Josh was practically born with a football in his hand. He knew how to throw a football before he knew how to talk. Football had always been his passion, while Steve had been forced into it.

Kristin was sitting on the white, mink rug, while Josh was sitting in her desk chair. She had a piece of paper out to jot the ideas down. So far, it was blank except for the small doodles Kristin had drawn out of boredom. They both stared into space. Kristin's laptop beeped, notifying her that someone had messaged her. It was at her desk in front of Josh. She was too lazy to get up to read it, so she asked Josh to do it. He opened her laptop. Kristin was surprised that Josh still remembered the password to her laptop. He was the only person she had ever trusted enough to tell her password to besides Elizabeth, of course. Josh opened the message and told Kristin that the message was from Steve. He was apologizing for the way he behaved at his house, and apparently, his date went well. Most importantly, he asked Kristin if she still wanted to be his "friend date" to the Halloween party.

"Are you going to say yes?" Josh asked her. There was a bit of reluctance in his voice, as if he wanted an answer, but he was scared of what it would be.

Kristin chose her next words carefully. "I don't know, should I? I know it's completely weird for me to be asking you, but you and I are just getting back to a solid friendship. I wouldn't want to make you uncomfortable by going with your friend. So if you don't want me to go I'm okay with that."

"Kristin, it's not about me. Do you want to go with him? Do you like him? Jesus, girl, get your feelings together."

Kristin groaned. "I don't really know. I mean I think so. Will you be at the party? Sorry that was a stupid question. Of course you will be; you're the star of the team." Kristin laughed nervously.

Josh smiled. Josh started typing away. When Kristin asked what he was doing, he told her he was writing a reply to Steve saying, Of course. He then said, "And that wasn't a stupid question. My mom's actually having a fund-raising gala that night."

"That sounds nice," Kristin replied while smiling. She imagined Josh dressed to the nines in a well-fitted suit, mingling with all the fancy business people.

"I guess. All those rich, business people are be so fake though. And you know how much I hate having to pretend that I like them just because they're my mom's 'friends'."

Kristin said, "Hey, look on the bright side. At least you get to see your mom. And I bet some of your other family members will be there, too, right?"

"That's true. You're right, it will be kind of fun. If you weren't going to the Halloween party with Steve, I'd ask you to go with me. You know my family loves you. They ask about you all the time." Josh looked down at his Nike shoes.

Kristin smiled a little when she thought of Josh's family. They were all so sweet and down to earth, despite the lavish lifestyle they lived. He continued, "But, he beat me to it so that's all done with. Now, how are we going to get the entire school to side with you? Your cute face can get you a lot, but I don't know if it's enough to sell the whole school."

"I guess if I simply state my case and explain my side of the story that will be enough."

"Eliza has a lot of power. If she wants to convince everyone at school that you're guilty, she can do it. Sure, telling your side will help. You need to win this thing. The best way to do that is with evidence. Get ready to do some serious snooping if Edwards approves the trial."

"Okay. My mom will be coming home from work soon. You better get going. If she sees you here she will interrogate me all night about whether there's anything going on between us. Plus, I've got a lot of homework to do. So do you."

Josh replied, "You're right. See you tomorrow? I can pick you up in the morning. Maybe stop at Starbucks for breakfast?"

"Umm, I'll let you know in the morning?"

"All right. Thanks for having me over."

"No, thank you for helping me."

Josh leaned in to hug her.

Surprisingly, she hugged back. She embraced his strong arms and the good smell of his cologne. Kristin missed his hugs, they made her feel safe. Before she let herself get too wrapped up in his charm, she pulled back. "Bye, J," she whispered.

"Bye, sweetheart." Josh kissed her on the cheek before walking out of her room.

When he walked out of the room, Kristin let herself fall back onto her bed. Did Josh just kiss her? Even if it was on the cheek, it had to have meant something. After all, he had pretty much admitted his affection for her at school. It was all becoming too much. Could she be falling for him again? The first time she fell for him she had not braced herself for heartbreak. Back then, he could do no wrong in her eyes. Everything about him was perfect, from the way he said her name, to the way he laughed. Before she knew it, she had turned into one of those girls who claimed that the felt "butterflies." She was sure he would have never, ever hurt her. He did everything right, from randomly bringing her flowers or even expensive jewelry to planning romantic dinner dates on his family yacht. However, Josh could appreciate the simpler things in life as well. Sure, he was extremely wealthy but, that did not mean that they did not do normal things. Kristin and Josh did things such as going on walks down by the lake near his house, strolling through downtown, and having movie nights in his basement.

Kristin could remember vividly the first date he took her on. She was in a pink fit and flare mini dress with white stilettos. When they arrived at the restaurant, Kristin noticed that no one was there.

"Why is it so empty?" she wondered, when they entered the place.

"I rented the entire thing out," Josh replied. A waiter showed them to a private room where candles were set up everywhere, along with red roses.

"No one has ever done something like this for me," she stated. She found herself unable to stop looking around. It was all so beautiful. She could tell that a lot of thought had been put into it. Her voice showed exactly what she was feeling, amazement. Her mouth hung open in shock.

"Well, you deserve it. You look extremely beautiful tonight, by the way." Josh pulled out her chair like a gentleman and he placed her jacket on the back of her chair for her. "Let's check out the menu. You ever been here before?"

"Nope. You?"

"I've come here a couple times with my parents but never for a date. It looks like the lamb chops could be good. See anything you like?"

Kristin gasped. "Everything is so expensive. You don't have to buy this fancy stuff for me. Don't get me wrong, it's a really nice thought but I don't want to be a burden."

"Kristin, I've got enough money in my trust fund to buy the entire state of Michigan. I want to do something nice for you. When you're with me, you can get whatever you like. I like you a lot. And before you say something I've heard before, everything is not about money with me."

"So you didn't ask me out because I'm rich?"

"Of course not."

"You'd date me if I had two cents to my name?"

"Absolutely."

"Well, I think you should know that I was not always rich. Money is still sort of a new thing for me. I'm not like you. You've had a silver spoon in your mouth since you came out your mother's womb. You probably took private tennis lessons at some elite country club when you were five, right?" Kristin wondered.

"My dad is not in my life. He walked out on my mom, my little sister, and I when I was twelve. So, yes, maybe I was born with a silver spoon but I've had it snatched away from me. When my dad left, he also took his money with him. His side is the rich one. My mom was forced to get into the workforce. She built an empire from nothing. Oh no, I didn't ask you out because of your money. I asked you out because you seem like an intelligent, funny, and most definitely stunning girl."

"Wow, I'm so sorry for even insulting you like that," Kristin apologized.

"It's fine."

"And Josh?"

"Yeah?"

"I like you, too."

Kristin felt herself smile as she thought of their first date. They'd spent the rest of the night laughing and getting to know each other. She found him to be just the right amount of charming and sweet. It was absolutely perfect. Pretty much everything Josh said and did was perfect. He was polite to her mother, sweet all the time. He was not afraid to show his affection in public. He was a dream come true but, it's a common fact that all good things come to an end. And her and Josh's end was a nasty, bitter one.

"Am I actually starting to like him again? Am I even seriously asking myself this again?" Kristin wondered.

"Are you asking yourself what again?" her mother asked.

Kristin jumped instinctively. She had not even heard her mother enter the house.

"When did you get here?"

"Two moments ago. Are you okay? You seem weird."

Kristin sat up on her bed. "I'm not. I didn't even hear you enter the house."

"Josh was leaving as I was coming in. By the way, why was he here?"

Kristin quickly came up with a suitable lie. "Well, um...he wanted to come and pick up something he never got me after our breakup."

"Really? He seemed really happy when I saw him."

"Hmm...Maybe he was just happy to have it back."

"Well, what was it?"

Kristin quickly replied, "Something very, very personal. Mother, I'd love to chat, but I've honestly got so much homework."

"Why are you blushing?" Her mother put her hand on her hip and raised a brow.

Kristin covered her cheeks with her hands. "I'm not! Now, shoo! Shoo!" She got up from her bed and closed the door in her mother's face.

"*This day has been crazy,*" Kristin thought before getting started on her homework.

Chapter 13
You've Got One Chance

Kristin lay in her soft, silky sheets curled up into a ball. Her soft comforter was placed across her. A history textbook was next to her. She had fallen asleep while reviewing the chapter they'd been assigned for homework. Thank God that she changed into her pajamas before she started studying. Her phone began ringing. With her eyes still closed, she used her hand to feel around on her nightstand for her phone. Finally, she grabbed it. Bringing it over to her ear, Kristin opened one eye to accept the call.

"Hey?" Josh said as soon as the phone stopped ringing. The extreme perkiness in his voice made her jump a little.

"Josh, what the heck are you doing calling me this early? What is it? Two in the morning?"

Josh informed, "No, it's seven. School starts in an hour in a half."

"I don't care. I'm very tired. Now, if you'll excuse me, I'm going back to sleep. Good-"

"Wait! I have a surprise. Look outside your window."

"I swear if you're outside my house with a dozen red roses— "

"No, I brought you breakfast. I thought you'd need some energy today."

Kristin snapped into the phone, "I don't care. I'm going back to bed."

"So you're just going to leave me outside your house?"

"If my mom finds out you're here, I'm dead. I already told you she'll interrogate me about you and I until I give her answers."

"Please? I'll be quiet. We can eat in your room. I was trying to do a nice thing for my friend."

"Ugh!" Kristin ended the call before letting out another groan. Of course she appreciated Josh's sweet gesture; she just wished he would have done it when she didn't feel and look like crap. She got out of bed and slipped on her Ugg slippers. Kristin was extra careful not to make any noise when she walked down the steps, so that she did not wake her mother.

Kristin swung open the door. She was still wearing her pajamas, which included shorts and a tank top. She quickly skimmed him. His dark wash skinny jeans fit him nicely, and he paired it a short-sleeved Ralph Lauren Polo that showed off his perfectly sculpted arms. She tried not to look interested in him, but she could not help it. It seemed like Josh was getting more and more good-looking with time.

"You look hot," Josh said. He gave her a smooth wink.

Kristin didn't want him to know how flattered she was, so she rolled her eyes and pretended to be grossed out. "Eww," she replied.

"Oh, please. Don't act like you weren't just checking me out. Yeah, I noticed," he said smoothly.

"You *wish* I was checking you out!" Kristin exclaimed, "Now, come in. I'm actually kind of hungry. And be extra quiet. My mom is asleep."

"I'm not giving you the food until you admit that I look hot today," Josh stated. Kristin gave him a look. "I'm serious," he said.

She said in a monotone voice, "Josh, you look hot today."

Josh handed her the bag of food and entered her house. They ate in her room and watched re-runs of *Drake & Josh* together. Kristin indulged in a caramel macchiato and a cheese croissant. Afterwards, Josh helped her pick out her outfit for school. He'd always had a great sense of style. That was one of the perks of having him as a boyfriend– he was a boyfriend and a personal stylist. Kristin had gotten ready quickly so that they could sneak out of her house before her mother woke up. She wrote her mother a note saying that one of her friends had picked her up to go get breakfast. The ride to school was a quiet one. Kristin always got quiet when she was extremely nervous. Josh did his best to help her calm down. When they got to school, he wished her good luck on her meeting with Principle Edwards. They parted ways, as he went to his locker and she went to the office.

Kristin waited anxiously in a chair. She played with the hem of her plaid skirt.

Moments later, Principle Edwards came out of his office, looking stressed as ever. "Come on back, Kristin," he told her. When they got back into his office, she took a seat. Her backpack sat on the floor next to her chair. "So, I assume you did not find a way to prove yourself."

"Actually, I kind of did."

Principal Edwards looked surprised. "You did?"

"I did."

He wondered, "What exactly did you come up with?"

She began, "This school is supposed to be a place where the students thrive and make key decisions that can make this school even better. We, the students, are supposed to essentially be leaders of not only the school, but the entire community. Correct?" Principal Edwards nodded in response, looking intrigued. Kristin continued confidently, "I think that since the students are the ones who make up the school, they should be the ones who can decide whether or not I can stay. I was thinking of a trial."

Principal Edwards seemed to catch on to what she was leaning towards. "So, you'd get a chance to convince them and sell your case?"

"Exactly. I'd be the defense, the school would be the jury, and I guess the prosecutor would be whoever wants to go against me. And you'd be the judge, of course."

"Okay. I'm a little reluctant to go through with this trial thing, but it seems pretty fair. Kristin, you must understand that if majority of the people vote against you..."

Kristin swallowed, "I'll have to leave the school."

"Yes. How about if we have the trial this Friday? Sound good?"

"Friday? I guess that's fine. I'll have a quick assembly later on today telling everyone about the trial."

"Thank you."

"You've got one chance. Savor it."

Chapter 14
Jealous

Kristin and Josh were sitting outside on the school's lawn eating their lunch. The school lawn was a popular place during lunch. Around them, everyone was talking. Much to Kristin's delight, they weren't gossiping about her. Kristin was just happy that Eliza and her evil minions were nowhere to be found. She had not seen Eliza all day, surprisingly. She told Josh about the meeting with Principle Edwards. He was almost just as excited as she was. Kristin wondered where Steve was; she had not seen him all day. She thought that since he had asked her to that Halloween party, he would at least say hi to her but, he was nowhere to be found. Before Kristin and Josh had decided to go outside and eat lunch, she had insisted that he sit with his football friends. Josh had told her that it was not really a big deal and that they wouldn't even notice that he was gone.

They conversed casually as they ate. Kristin vented to him about his Bio test. Josh vented to her about the football team's upcoming game against their rival school. Apparently, he had been practicing and training harder than ever–working out for hours, watching nothing but football, studying the other team's film and sticking to a strict diet his nutritionist had put him on to make sure he was in the best shape of his life for the game. That meant no more fast food. Kristin was so impressed by his tenacity. He really was working hard towards his dream. Strange as it may sound, Kristin admired Josh. Sure, he had his slight faults, but he was an incredible person.

"I'm proud of you, Josh. I just want you to know that," Kristin told him. She put her hand on him and patted him on the back.

He smiled cheekily. "Thank you. That means a lot to me. By the way, I was thinking we could do some snooping today. Ya know, for evidence? We can be like secret spy agents. You could get a cute, all black jumpsuit. Kinda like cat woman, ya know?" He wriggled his eyebrows flirtatiously. "I've always wanted to be an FBI agent. I don't know if I've told you this story, but this one time when I was ten I had a dream where I was this super cool agent–kinda like James Bond only cooler and I was in France when–"

Kristin cut him off. "You've told me the story, Josh, about ten times. Now, how exactly are we going to snoop for evidence?"

"There's only one person in this school who knows everything about everybody, and that person also probably has the numbers of everyone in the school," Josh said.

"Eliza," they both said at the exact same time.

Josh said, "I was thinking maybe we could hack her email or steal her phone. Maybe there's something in there about whatever happened with the dodgeball."

"And how exactly will we get her phone?" Kristin asked with a hint of doubt in her voice.

"I'll distract her with my good looks and flirting skills, while you get her phone."

"And if nothing's in her phone?" Kristin asked.

"We'll cross that bridge when and if we get there," he said. He looked up and saw Steve. "Looks like Steve is coming our way." Josh gestured in his direction. Kristin froze up at the sight of him. Soon, he was standing right over her.

"Hey, Josh. Hey, Kristin, can I talk to you for a minute?"

"Sure. Go ahead."

Steve tensed up a bit. The sun was gleaming down on his face, making him even more attractive. Kristin still couldn't decide which guy was more attractive: Josh or Steve. Steve was instantly hot, there was no denying that. And, Josh was too. There was something about Josh's perfect smile that made him innocently irresistible. He had always had some weird type of hold on her.

Steve replied, "I'd actually like to talk to you alone. If that's okay with Josh?"

Josh hesitantly said, "That's cool, man. I'm actually just about to go to class. Kristin, I'll text you later... for the thing." Josh winked before standing up.

Kristin stood up as well. She figured she should repay Steve for making her jealous of the girl at the party. "Wait, Josh," Kristin said flirtatiously. "You can't leave without a goodbye hug."

Josh looked completely taken aback. He furrowed his brows a bit in confusion. However, he leaned in and gave her a hug.

As they were hugging, he whispered, "I know you're trying to make Steve jealous. We will definitely be talking about this later."

"Thank you," she whispered back.

Once Josh had gone inside, things got awkward between Kristin and Steve. She felt nervous around him for some reason, but not just because he was a jock. Could it be possible that Kristin was starting to develop feelings for Steve and Josh? Obviously, her feelings for Josh were much more complicated.

"Since when were you and Josh so cool with each other again?" Steve asked her.

"We're friends. Are you jealous?"

Steve replied, "Yeah, I am. I'm pretty good friends with Josh and it's very awkward. I thought you were pissed at him because he cheated."

"Don't you dare bring that up."

"I'm sorry," Steve apologized. "I just feel like he hurt you so badly. You're way too amazing to have to sit there and just accept someone who doesn't even respect you."

"What are you getting at?"

"He doesn't deserve you. He had his chance and he proved that he's a total douche bag," Steve said.

"Do not say that about him. You don't know anything about Josh or our relationship. You don't understand anything about Josh and I. And we aren't even together."

"Look, I went on that date with the girl from the party. Truth be told, she and I have no connection. She's not *half* the girl you are. I told her that I won't be seeing her again. want you. I know you said that you wanted to be friends, but I cannot be friends. Kristin, I know that you like me too. Admit it."

"Okay, fine. I like you," Kristin said with a smile.

"What about Josh?"

Kristin inhaled sharply. "Josh and I have nothing except a friendship," she said, even though she was not sure if it was true. She still got butterflies whenever Josh was around.

"Cool. So, you'll be going to the Halloween party with me as my date?"

"Yes." Kristin and Steve smiled nervously at each other and he put her hand in his. As they held hands, he walked her to her next class.

Towards the end of the day, the assembly had taken place. Hundreds of students rushed into the gym. It was more crowded than rush hour. Everyone was chattering and wondering what was going on. Kristin sat in the crowd next to Steve. She spotted Josh across the room. When he happened to look up and lock eyes with her, she quickly looked away. Steve had his arm wrapped his arm around Kristin's shoulder. They would have been on the same side of the gym as Josh and the rest of the other football players, but by the time they had gotten to the gym it was packed. Plus, Kristin did not feel comfortable hanging out with the team. She had become friends with quite a few of them while she was with Josh, but those friendships became awkward after the breakup. Kristin looked around the gym for Elizabeth. It didn't take long before she heard the obnoxious cackle of Eliza, and sure enough, Elizabeth was right next to her. Principal Edwards explained the trial idea to the entire school. Many of the students seemed skeptical but Kristin was sure that she could get them onboard with the idea. Of course Eliza had volunteered to go against Kristin in the trial. It was announced that the trial would take place in the school auditorium at the very beginning of the school day. Kristin knew that she did not have much time to build her case but she was confident that she and Josh could be successful. And, who knows? Maybe Steve could even help them.

Chapter 15
Secret Agents

"**Okay**, here's the plan to swipe Eliza's phone. You ready to hear it?" Kristin asked. They were standing in the janitor's closet after school. Kristin thought that if they discussed the plan anywhere else, someone would end up hearing them. It was so dark in there that Kristin could barely even see Josh's face. Josh knew that Kristin was still slightly afraid of the dark, so he had used his phone as a flashlight. Kristin was a little shocked by this gesture; he always teased her about it. Then again, he had been making efforts to get on her good side. Bringing her breakfast, helping her with the whole plan thing; he definitely was trying. Kristin appreciated that.

"Wait, what happened with Steve?" Josh questioned.

Kristin couldn't decide whether or not to tell Josh the truth. A part of her wanted to fully open up to him again, but another part of her knew that Steve was right about Josh. Josh had hurt her in a way that no one had ever hurt her before. He should consider himself lucky that she had forgiven him. She then considered everything he had recently done for her. She at least owed it to him to be truthful. "Well, we finally both admitted our feelings for each other." Kristin saw Josh force a smile.

"That's great," he said. Despite his words, Josh's tone was less than enthusiastic. Kristin tried her best to ignore it. Maybe she was just hearing things.

"Yeah. We can talk about that later, though. Now, here's the plan: You'll go up to Eliza and distract her with your "flirtiness" and good looks. You'll tell her that you want to talk to her outside," Kristin explained.

"Wait a minute, did you say that I have good looks?"

Kristin bluffed, "It was a joke." Josh laughed hysterically. Kristin could not believe she had actually admitted his attractiveness for the second time in one day.

Josh said, "Tell me I'm amazingly hot, or I won't go along with the plan."

Kristin just glared at him. Was he serious? Why did he need her to say it? Hadn't he been flattered enough when she admitted it while he was standing at her doorstep? Back when they were together, she told him he was good-looking all the time. Everyone always told him how handsome he was—even adults. Kristin thought about it for a moment. Maybe she could make a compromise with Josh. "I'll give you one compliment," she said.

There was a small silence.

"Okay, fine, Josh said."

"Okay. Well." Kristin fumbled with the hem of her shirt. She couldn't think of the right words to express what she was thinking. "Um," she stammered. She looked up at Josh to find him waiting anxiously. "Your eyes," she finally said, "Your eyes are amazing. They have this glow." Another silence. Neither of them said anything for a while. Kristin could feel the tension in the room getting weird, so she tried to get back on task. "Anyway, back to the plan. So, while you're talking to her, I'll be trying to get her phone out of her locker, which is where you'll make sure she puts it before you take her outside and distract her. As soon as you have her outside, text me. I'll stay here in the closet till then. Oh, and I'll swipe her phone from her locker, and then as soon as I get it I will send you a text message–from her phone. Got it?"

"How will you know her combo?"

"I know it from when we were friends."

"Okay. Wish me good luck," he said before exiting the closet.

Kristin let out a huge sigh. They were going to need more than luck for this to work. Eliza was pretty clever. Hopefully, she would not suspect anything. Kristin remained in the closet, while Josh approached Eliza, who was talking with all her friends near her locker. One minute passed, then another, and then another. Kristin was starting to get restless. She was slightly claustrophobic, and there was something about janitors' closets that had always creeped her out. Maybe it was the fact that she'd seen way too many of those Lifetime murder mysteries. What was taking Josh so long? What if Eliza had managed to charm him enough that he actually became interested? No, that couldn't be. Josh knew what type of person Eliza was. Kristin did her best to keep busy while the time passed. She played games on her phone, looked at some celebrity gossip sites, and checked social media. After about fifteen minutes, Josh texted her saying she was good to go. Kristin slipped out of the janitor's closet. She looked in both directions of the hallway. There was no one in sight. Kristin walked to Eliza's locker and opened it. While she was getting Eliza's cell out, one of Eliza's puppets appeared.

"What are you doing?" the girl quipped.

Kristin jumped out of shock. She turned around. "Nothing."

"Something's up," she stated. "I'm telling Eliza!" She turned to walk away.

Kristin grabbed her arm. She threatened, "If you tell Eliza, I'll tell everyone in school that you had lip injections last week." The girl's jaw dropped. "That's right, I know." A smile spread across Kristin's lips.

"Fine." The girl ran off, leaving Kristin alone in the hallway again. She looked around to make sure no one was watching. Once the coast was clear, Kristin opened Eliza's locker again and got her phone. She texted Josh that the plan had been successful and headed to his car to wait for him.

Chapter 16
Chinese Take-Out and Lots of Texting

Josh and Kristin laughed hysterically at a corny joke he had just told. Kristin gripped her stomach. She was laughing so hard that it actually had begun to hurt. They were sitting on the floor of her room. Soft blankets were spread out under them. Josh was going through all of Eliza's emails, texts, and chats. Kristin was sitting across from him, eating Chinese take-out that Josh had ordered for them. He knew it was one of Kristin's guilty pleasures.

Kristin said, "This shrimp fried rice is so good. I think I'm going to eat all of it." She groaned loudly.

"Is that a good thing?" he wondered.

She said, "It's a good thing for my taste buds, but not for my thighs." She straightened up, suddenly felt a little self-conscious.

"Don't even say that. You're perfect. There's not an ounce of fat on your body," Josh told her.

Kristin gave a small smile. Venting to Josh about her flaws was pointless. All he would say in return was that she was perfect the way she was.

In Kristin's eyes, she was not perfect. She was pretty, but not overwhelmingly beautiful or as she would call it: scary pretty. You see, there were some people whose beauty was so immense and whose features were so sharp that it was scary but in a good way. The type of people that when you saw them for the first time you had to do a double take. To be honest, she was kind of happy about that. She didn't want to be the one to make others faint. Josh had always told her the exact opposite: that every time he saw her, his heart skipped a beat, as cliché as it may have sounded. Kristin decided to change topics. "Find anything in her phone yet?"

Josh didn't say anything. His eyebrows were scrunched together and his eyes were focused on the phone's screen.

Kristin tried to read his facial expression. She pushed, "Tell me."

"There are some emails between Eliza and Portia. The subject of the emails is "our little secret." Sounds fishy, right?"

Kristin said, "Totally. Let me see!" She took the phone from Josh's hands. As she read, Kristin couldn't believe her eyes. How could Eliza have been so stupid not to delete the emails? Kristin explained her findings to Josh. "In the emails, Eliza says that her plan is going great, and that no one will find out about the "dodgeball secret." And Eliza also said that Elizabeth is so gullible."

Josh's face lit up with excitement. "Wow, this agent stuff is pretty easy."

"Don't get too excited. In the emails, Eliza didn't exactly say that she threw the dodgeball, or that she had anything to do with it. We need more evidence." Kristin's phone began ringing. Kristin quickly looked at the screen. Kristin felt herself stiffen a bit. "It's Steve," she told Josh before answering. "Hello?" Kristin had a full smile on her face.

Josh noticed the smile, and was sure that Steve could even hear the smile through the phone. Why did it have to be Steve who made Kristin smile?

"Hey, Kristin. I was wondering if you needed any help with the trial?"

"Yes, I would love that actually. Can you come now?" she asked. She looked over to Josh. He feigned a smile. Kristin knew Josh well enough to be able to recognize when he was being fake. "Great, be there in fifteen."

Kristin and Josh sat in her room talking, waiting for to Steve showed up. Kristin could easily tell that Josh was not thrilled about Steve coming. She hated the fact that she had come between their friendship. Why did things have to be so complicated? Josh liked her. Steve liked her. Kristin liked Steve. Everything was so overwhelming.

Out of the blue Josh said, "You never told me why you had to make Steve jealous."

"I just wanted him to feel the way I felt when he was all over that girl."

Josh stated, "You really like him."

"I do, I'm just scared."

"About what?" Josh asked.

"I don't want him to hurt me. I haven't dated anyone since–"

Josh finished, "Since me."

Kristin nodded.

"I know that I hurt you. I have not been the same since what went down but, I promise you that I did not mean to. There's no need to be afraid of dating. You're an amazing person. You'll meet some guy who loves you."

"I don't think anyone can love me the way you did," Kristin said. She felt so vulnerable. Saying things out loud was challenging enough. Saying them to Josh was just icing on the cake.

"They can, and they will. Any guy would be extremely fortunate to have you in their life."

"But what if I do get hurt? What if I end up crying all the time over him? I don't want to go through that again."

"Again?" When Kristin nodded her head, Josh felt awful. He had made her cry. Their breakup had really cut her deeply. "I'm sorry I made you cry like that. I had my share of sleepless nights too."

"Really?"

"Really," he said.

"What are we doing, Josh? We both know that we're just leading each other on. Eventually we're going to start falling for each other again. This is dangerous territory. *We* are dangerous territory."

Josh responded, "Maybe we are but what's wrong with that?"

"I can't fall for you because, the thing about you is that once someone has fallen for you, there's no chance of letting go. You get me in your trap, and then"

"You can't get out. I feel the exact same way about you."

Kristin felt herself getting emotional. "I'm sorry for getting all," she paused, "you know?"

"No, it's okay. C'mere. You need a hug," Josh said. Kristin got up and walked over to Josh. He sat her down in front of her and hugged her tightly. She tucked her head into his neck, which smelled of good cologne. "I'll always be here for you. Don't cry. You're too pretty for that." He started to say those three words that he was once accustomed to saying to her. Something stopped him, though.

"Thank you so much."

He said, "No problem."

Kristin said, "Let's make a promise. We will never get romantically involved with each other again. Okay?"

"Okay. That's probably for the best anyway," Josh said. On the inside, he did not want to make that sort of promise but, he wanted most of all for Kristin to be happy. They locked pinkies and were still sitting on the floor.

"Knock, knock?" a voice asked from Kristin's doorway. Both Kristin and Josh whipped their heads around. There stood Steve. Kristin stood up, leaving Josh there. She ran up to him and they hugged. When they finally pulled away she still could not stop smiling. He said, "You look beautiful."

Kristin blushed and covered her face with her hands. Steve put his hands on top of hers and slowly pulled her hands from her face. "Thank you," she finally said, "You do, too." Kristin then realized what she had said. "I mean, you look handsome. I'm sorry!"

"It's fine. I know what you meant, babe."

Kristin nearly fell over when she heard him utter the word. "By the way, sorry we didn't get to spend a lot of time together at school today." Steve put her hand in his. Josh sat on the floor awkwardly.

"That's okay," Kristin said quietly. In all honesty, she was not that sad about it. Lunch with Josh had been fun.

Josh said, "We found some emails between Eliza and Portia. Eliza said that Elizabeth was "gullible" and that her plan was working. We need more, though. The emails weren't specific enough."

"You need an alibi," Steve said.

"I don't have one. I was there when Elizabeth got knocked out. There's really no way to prove that I didn't do it without proving that someone else did."

Josh told her, "I can take Eliza's phone home and hook it up to my computer, and then print out the emails. That way, if Eliza ever finds out that we took her phone, we'll have the hard evidence."

"That'll be great," Kristin said.

"What about me? What am I supposed to do?" Steve asked the both of them.

Josh rolled his eyes.

"Work on Elizabeth," Kristen said. If we can get her to be on our side, she can do some searching for us. After all, she and Eliza are close now. They're around each other all the time. I'll try to get her to talk to me too."

"This just might work," Josh said.

Chapter 17
This Doesn't Feel Right

Kristin felt a tingly feeling in her stomach. Watching Elizabeth laugh her head off with Eliza and her snobby friends made her feel sad. Besides, Elizabeth was not even laughing for real. It was a fake laugh. Kristin wanted her best friend back. Eliza had plenty of people to hang out with. Why did she have to pick Elizabeth? Plus, if Eliza really had wanted to remain friends with Elizabeth, then she would never had ostracized Elizabeth and Kristin from her group of friends. She had done so in November of ninth grade, which was about the time that Kristin and Josh had started to become closer.

Eliza had always been well-liked. She had been the most popular girl in school from pre-kindergarten to fourth grade. In fourth grade, when Kristin came, Eliza started hanging out with her more. She was willing to not hang out with the other popular students whom she known all her life, so that she could be friends with Kristin and Elizabeth. Eliza didn't mind. Her "friends," however, did mind. They had always begged her to stop being friends with Kristin and Elizabeth. For some reason, in ninth grade, she finally accepted their offer. She threw Kristin and Lizzie to the side. Both of them had no idea how to cope with losing a friend they'd had for years. Kristin begged Eliza numerous times to talk to them, but Eliza said that she was over them and moving on to bigger and better things.

Kristin still felt better about the situation. She'd lost a friend. Eliza started being intentionally mean to Elizabeth and Kristin. Kristin never understood that. If Eliza decided that she was no longer with them, that was one thing but torturing them? That was plain mean.

The time when it hurt Kristin the most not to have Eliza as a friend was when Josh and Kristin broke up. Eliza had always been closer to Kristin than Elizabeth. They were like sisters. She could have definitely used her advice during that time period. After her breakup with Josh, Kristin never wanted to do anything. It was hard enough for her to get out of bed every day, but it was even harder for her to go to school and face Josh. He seemed to be everywhere, and she always had to put on a brave face and pretend that everything was all right. Eliza knew what Kristin was going through, but that was not enough to make her be nice to Kristin. The only people that had really been of assistance to Kristin were her mother and Elizabeth.

While Kristin was watching Elizabeth and Eliza talk, an idea popped into her head. Maybe if she were to text some of Eliza's friends from Eliza's phone, she could get them to reveal some information. They would think it was Eliza, right? Today was Tuesday. The trial was on Friday, as well as the Halloween party. Kristin decided that she would only go to the party if she won the trial. What would be the point in going to the party of the school's team if she was no longer a part of the school?

"Do you want your breadsticks?" Steve asked.

Kristin was brought out of her thinking and back into the real world. "No. Go ahead," Kristin said. Kristin looked across the room and saw Josh at the football table. She'd practically forced him to go sit with his friends. He had tried to be resistant, but Kristin knew that even though he liked hanging with her, he had to have missed his other friends too.

"I'm excited about the party. It'll be our first real date," he said.

Kristin smiled. It was a fake smile, but Steve did not know her well enough to tell that it was not real.

"Yeah, me too."

Chapter 18
Snooping (Again)

"I'm starting to think that I'm in your room way too often," Josh said. Again, they were sitting in her room on the floor. They decided they were going to text Portia from Eliza's phone when Steve showed up. Until then, Josh filled her in on the football team drama. Kristin was fascinated by the fact that even guys had drama. She was also proud of Josh because, according to what he had told her, he had managed to stay out of the drama for the most part. He also told her that a lot of his friends had been pressuring him to find a girlfriend. He said that he felt left out of the group sometimes, because they all had girlfriends. Kristin assured him that he would find someone, as long as he was open-minded. Josh even admitted that he had gone on a date a couple weeks ago.

"And how did that go?" Kristin wondered. When Josh burst into laughter, she knew what the answer was. "What? She wasn't pretty enough for you?"

Josh said, "No, she was beautiful." Kristin raised an eyebrow. "She was really pretty. We just didn't have a connection. It's so frustrating."

Kristin explained to Josh that he could not rush it. She told him that everything would fall into place at the right time. Despite their harsh breakup, she knew Josh was a good guy. He was sweet and extremely thoughtful. Practically every girl at school fell to his feet. He could have a girlfriend in a heartbeat, but finding one that was worthy would be a challenge. He also told her about the fact that he wished he had a father to talk about that type of stuff with. Kristin couldn't help but feel bad for him. Even though both their fathers weren't around, with him it was different. He'd never even met his father. He'd left them when Josh was just a baby. When they were dating, he always vented about it. Kristin assured him that one day his father would come back. If he didn't, that was his loss. He'd just never know how amazing his son was.

"Thanks, Kristin," Josh said, "I really appreciate that."

"No problem," she said. They spent the rest of the time talking about random things—mostly their favorite restaurants. They were in the middle of an intense conversation about Chipotle's burritos when Steve rang the bell. They went down to greet him and then they all went upstairs to Kristin's room. There was an awkward silence in the room. Steve broke the silence by revealing some valuable information. Apparently, he had overheard a conversation between Eliza and Portia. They had been talking about the dodgeball incident.

According to Steve, Eliza had said that she needed to get Kristin out of the school for good. Portia had then told Eliza that "It could be done. As long as we can frame her." This, by sure, was the happiest news Kristin had received all day. It was exactly the evidence that she needed. Finally, they were on the right track.

"Are you serious?" Kristin exclaimed. "This is great, thank you so much, Steve. Oh my god, I'm so happy." She instantly wrapped her arms around him and began jumping up and down. Steve laughed and hugged her back.

"You're welcome."

Josh asked harshly, "Well, did you get it on tape? We can take your word for it, but the entire school can't."

Steve and Kristin untangled from each other. Kristin had never thought to ask about him recording the conversation, but it was a good question. Josh glared at Steve. Kristin slowly unwrapped her arms from around Steve's torso. She turned to Steve, anxious for his reply. Kristin pushed, "Well, did you get it on tape?" She looked hopefully at Steve.

"I didn't think of that," Steve said.

Kristin put her hands on her face in frustration. She couldn't believe that Steve had not recorded the conversation. They were so close to having all the evidence they needed, and just like that–they were back to square one.

"How did you not record it? Do you not understand that this is serious? If you really like Kristin the way you say that you do, you'll want to do everything you can to keep her happy. Isn't that what a good boyfriend is supposed to do?" Josh asked.

Kristin looked up, surprised at what he had said. She shot Josh a look. He avoided her gaze. Instead, he stared at Steve.

"I think it's pretty ironic for you to be saying that," Steve replied.

Josh scoffed, "What are you even talking about?"

"You think I don't know what you did to her? Cheating on her!"

"You told him?" Josh asked.

"Josh, it just—"

"Save it, Kris. Steve, you're not in any position to say that. You left Kristin to walk home by herself late at night. You put her safety in danger!" Josh fired.

Kristin finally got the courage to say something in the midst of their petty fighting. "Both of you, shut up!" She threw her hands in the air out of frustration. You're really getting on my nerves. Now, Steve...it's okay that you didn't record Portia and Eliza's conversation. It would have made things easier, but now that we know that Eliza is trying to frame me, all we have to do is get her to have another conversation like that with someone else. And then, we'll record it. Now, we just have to figure out a way to get her to say it again. Josh, you can flirt with her and get her to reveal some info. It's Tuesday, and the trial is in three days. We can do this." Kristin smiled.

Steve walked over to her and gave her a reassuring hug. She felt herself get all tingly. For some reason, being around Steve made her a little nervous. Besides Josh, she'd never had a serious relationship. Steve had not either, which made things easier. Oddly enough, when she hugged Steve, she could not help but think of when she hugged Josh a few minutes earlier. She suddenly felt angry at Josh. How was he managing to make her think of him even when she was in the arms of Steve? She was perfectly happy with Steve. She repeated the thought to herself again. She was perfectly happy with Steve.

"I'm gonna go," Josh said. Kristin noticed that he was avoiding eye contact with her. She wanted to just go up to him and apologize to him for telling Steve all about their relationship, but she couldn't. She didn't want Steve thinking there was anything between her and Josh. She didn't want to do anything that would make Steve lose trust in her. They were in a good place right now. Josh would have to just stick it out accept the fact that she and Steve liked each other. He quickly grabbed his jacket before he began to walk out of Kristin's room.

"You sure, Josh?" Kristin asked. She didn't want him to be home alone. "You don't have to. I thought you wanted to help."

"I do. I just have to pick up Allison from her friend's house. She stayed with her friend this week to give me a break," Josh said.

"You've been taking care of Allison," Kristin concluded.

Josh nodded.

Kristin couldn't believe his selflessness. Taking care of a young child was hard even for an adult. She suddenly felt empathy for him. She said, "Josh, that's amazing. I never knew that you had so much responsibility. Caring for a five-year-old is not easy." Kristin looked down at her hands. When she and Josh were dating, Allison stayed with their Aunt Marcee, since his mother was always traveling. Josh would pick her up and spend the weekend with her.

"Well, I'm her big brother. She's my responsibility."

Kristin replied, "That's really sweet, Josh. Tell her I said hi, okay?"

"I will," he said.

"Bye," Kristin said as Josh walked out of her room. After Josh left, Kristin began writing an outline of her trial speech. She was having trouble coming up with words to write. Usually, she was good at those sort of things. This time, for some reason, she couldn't quite get it right. She would type something and then delete it seconds later. So far, the only line that she had written down was "Hi, I'm Kristin Gregory." She fiddled with her pencil, twirling it around in her hands over and over. She then tapped it against her desk. The nerve-wracking noise was the only sound in the room. It echoed throughout her room.

Steve was sitting on her bed watching her struggle to find the right words to say. He walked over to her desk and wrapped his arm around her shoulder. "Don't worry, Kristin," he said kindly.

Kristin forced a smile. "I'm not worrying."

"I can see it in your face that you're stressing about the speech, and I just want to tell you not to. Everything will work out."

"Thanks," Kristin said, her voice suddenly becoming small. "Thanks for calming me down. And

I'm sorry for Josh acting all snappy. He's going through a lot, he just doesn't want to show it." She felt her heart sink as she thought of how hard his life was.

"Well, that might be true, but he still doesn't have to be rude. I can tell he still has feelings for you."

Kristin did not know how to reply to Steve's statement. She took a deep breath before talking. "There's a lot of history between Josh and I," she explained, "I'm always going to have a small place in my heart for him. I love Josh, but I," she paused, "I am not in love with him."

"Do you promise that you don't like him anymore?" Steve asked.

Kristin felt her body go numb. A question like that was such a deep one; a simple 'yes' or 'no' just would not comply. Kristin knew that the only way for she and Steve to have a future was for her to tell him what he wanted to hear, at least when it came to Josh. "Yes," she said.

He smiled at her and kissed her cheek. Kristin could almost feel a weight being lifted off Steve's shoulders. They sat in silence for a while. Kristin's head lay on Steve's shoulders. "My dad wants me home before dinner. I hope you don't mind if I have to go early?"

"Oh, no that's fine," Kristin said.

"See you later, babe," Steve said. He smiled, showing his perfect, white teeth.

Kristin melted at the word "babe." Maybe Steve was the one. It was obviously a little too early to tell, but Kristin had a weird feeling that he was her destiny. She went to bed that night with a smile on her face.

Chapter 19
Sandwiches with Tea

Kristin and Steve had decided to go to his house for lunch. The school cafeteria was offering its famous sloppy joe for lunch that day, which was famous for all the wrong reasons. Kristin sat across from him at his dining room table. The room was so big that she was sure she could fit her whole entire class in it. The table was perfectly set with elaborate china plates, carefully placed napkins, and beautiful glasses. In front of her was a turkey sandwich on one of Steve's elaborate plates. For some reason, she felt like she did not have a care in the world. This, obviously, was not true. It was Wednesday, and she still did not have any solid evidence against Eliza. Josh had promised that by the end of the day he would get information that would be useful. Kristin could only hope. Hanging with Steve and Josh was fun, but she missed her best friend. No guy could take the place of Elizabeth. It had been torture watching her flounce around casually with Eliza and her minions. Elizabeth seemed to always be laughing when she was with them. Kristin knew that she was the one who should have been laughing with Elizabeth. Lizzie was her best friend. Why did she have to rub it in Kristin's face that she was friends with Eliza now? Kristin wanted more than anything to go up to her and apologize to her for everything. Whenever she and Elizabeth made eye contact, she got the feeling that Elizabeth no longer wanted anything to do with her. Maybe their friendship was over for good. If that was the case, Kristin didn't know why she was even bothering with the trial. Going to school would be hell if she had no friends.

"What's wrong?" Steve asked.

Kristin said quickly, "I just miss Elizabeth. No big deal."

"I promise that she'll come around, especially when we show her Eliza's true colors."

Kristin began, "That's what's so shocking! She's already seen Eliza's true colors for herself. This August, when school started, Eliza treated us both like dirt! What she did was despicable and disgusting and horrific and mean and every other bad word I can think of. I just don't get it."

Kristin exhaled loudly. She tore all the ends off of her sandwich. Steve did not say anything. She wanted him to offer some sweet words and tell her that everything would be okay. Instead, he stuffed his sandwich into his mouth. She missed her mother, too. She'd been working at the studio even later than usual and by the time she got home, Kristin was already fast asleep. By the time Kristin woke up for school, her mother was either already at work or in a deep sleep. Kristin had pretty much been taking care of herself. Having to experience that made her feel even worse for Josh. She'd only been doing it for a few days, whereas he'd been doing it for years. Kristin picked up her sandwich and took a bite of it. She suddenly remembered how hungry she was. Steve watched her eat the sandwich ravenously.

They both ate in silence. It was so quiet one could hear a pen drop in the room. Kristin could not help but feel uncomfortable. There was an awkward silence in the room, and she did not know why. She hoped that Steve was not getting annoyed with all of her problems. She surely did not want him to think she was some damsel in distress who needed the help of guys all the time or maybe Steve just did not know what to say, she thought. Yeah, that was probably it. Steve had been pretty sweet to her lately. He seemed like he wanted to help her. Kristin assured herself that everything was fine between them. Obviously, he liked her. He had made that pretty clear. She looked across the table at Steve, admiring his face. He held the last remains of his sandwich in one hand, while his phone was held tightly by the other. He looked at the screen with a smile. It looked like he was texting. Kristin decided to pull her phone out to check if she had received any new messages. When she noticed the time, she gasped. They had to be back at school in five minutes in order to make it to their next class on time.

As if he was reading her mind, Steve said, "we'd better be getting back to school." While Steve took their plates back to the kitchen, Kristin gathered their stuff. They hurriedly walked out of the house and made their way to the car. Kristin looked at her reflection in the car mirror. She stood there with her hand on the door handle, glaring at herself. A feeling of disappointment washed over her. She was disappointed in the person she had been pretending to be over the past few months. If she had not been so concerned with the wrong things, maybe she would not be fighting a suspension and without her best friend. She sure hoped that Steve and Josh were right, and that Elizabeth would come around. Steve looked at Kristin from the inside of the car.

He gestured for her to get in. Kristin, on the other hand, was in a complete daze. He rolled the window down. "Kristin?" he called, "Are you going to get in?"

Kristin suddenly was brought back to Earth. She blinked a couple of times and then opened the door. As she buckled her seat belt, Steve began driving away from his house. "Sorry," she apologized. She saw Steve turn to look at her. "I was daydreaming. I'm just a little tired."

The car ride back was a short and quiet one. It was silent, but it was a comfortable silence. Kristin stared out the window as they sped down the street. She saw the first red leaf of the season. There was nothing prettier to her than the sight of warm colors on the trees' leaves. All the pretty reds, yellows, and oranges always seemed to make her feel better. As she absorbed the autumn atmosphere, she thought about the adventures she usually embarked on around this time of year. She and all her friends would go to the cider mills and haunted houses. She would give anything to be able to do that now. She looked over at Steve, who was focused on driving. The shining sun gently touched Steve's face, illuminating it. Kristin noticed how nice his side profile was. His nose was not too dominant or overpowering. It also wasn't a tiny, stub of a nose. It was just right.

Steve's car entered the school campus. There were students walking around, scurrying to get to class. Steve parked his car and they both quickly got out with their backpacks. The crisp, autumn air hit Kristin's skin. She folded her arms instinctively, trying to keep warm. Steve put her hand in his. As they walked across the school lawn to enter the building, Kristin made eye contact with Josh. He was standing on the lawn in a circle with all his friends. She saw his eyes darted to the hands of Steve and Kristin. He smiled a little and gave her a small wave. She slightly tilted her head to him. Steve walked her to her next class. When they reached her math class, they both stopped in front of the door.

"Have fun," he teased.

Kristin rolled her eyes. "Yeah, right," she replied.

The bell rang and students swarmed towards the classrooms. Kristin and Steve went their separate ways.

Halfway through math, Kristin went to the bathroom. She stood in the bathroom mirror. She stared at herself as she ran her fingers through her hair. After putting her hair into a ponytail, she reapplied her mascara. She stared at her forehead, noticing a few blemishes. Maybe it was time to go to the spa soon.

"Why can't I just be one of those perfect

models," she muttered. She frowned. Eliza emerged from one of the stalls. Kristin turned around in shock. She had not been aware that anyone else was in the bathroom. Eliza fixed her hair in the mirror. Kristin knew that one of Eliza's rituals was checking up on her reflection after lunch. They had always done that together when they were still friends.

"We all want to be perfect, Kris."

"You heard that?" Kristin asked.

"Models look perfect but are they really? Without all the makeup and airbrush, they're just like you and me. Have some self-confidence."

Kristin said, "Wow, Eliza. That was pretty profound for you. I didn't know you were so deep." She walked over to the sink and ran some water on her hands and gently ran her fingers through her pony. Her hair was so frizzy that day.

"Water doesn't help. I've told you that a million times." Eliza reached into her bag and pulled out some hair oil. "My mom just got this stuff for me from a beauty store. It helps with frizz. And, we both know how crazy my hair can get, so of course I have it with me at all times." She handed the bottle to Kristin. Kristin gave her a skeptical look before taking the bottle. "Oh, and don't think I don't know what you and Josh pulled." She paused and looked up while she re-considered what she had said. "Well, I guess I say what you *tried* to pull. You had him distract me by flirting, which he did horribly by the way. I had my phone service cancelled, just in case you guys tried to text any of my... allies. You have absolutely nothing on me." Eliza laughed before flipping her hair.

"Well, I will find something. Goodbye, Eliza."

Later that day, Kristin and Steve were holding hands as they walked down the hallway. A few people stared at them. Kristin was used to being stared at by now, so it did not feel as strange. When she and Josh had dated, it was like being a celebrity. Kristin had not started dating Josh because he was popular, but dating a popular jock had its perks. She had gained a lot of power when she and Josh became an official. But, Kristin always knew that it was never really her power, it was Josh's. At first, she was uncomfortable with all the attention. She wasn't used to it. Luckily, Josh was used to the attention and helped Kristin adjust. Once, she and Josh were eating lunch in the dining hall, and everyone was whispering about them.

"I feel so weird," Kristin told Josh, "Everyone keeps staring at us like we're Justin and Selena. This happens to you all the time, huh?"

"It took me awhile to get used to it all," he admitted. "Just act like they aren't looking. I like you a lot; I don't want you to get scared off."

"Has that happened to you before?"

"Yeah. I'll protect you, though. I've been dealing with this since I was little. It's not that bad."

"Seems like it. Don't worry, I won't get scared off. You're worth it."

Kristin had soon gotten used to dating a popular jock. At that point, she and Eliza were still friends. The more that Kristin thought about it, she realized that she was responsible for Eliza's social success. When Kristin was dating Josh, Eliza would hang out with them. That was initially how she was lured into the world of the "populars." At the time, Kristin had no real interest in becoming the head of the school; she was just enjoying her time with Josh. Speaking of Josh, he was coming their way.

"Hey," Josh greeted. He had his hands stuffed in his pockets. Kristin looked at his eyes. Though they were sparkling as usual, they were not as bright. His voice was also a little scruffy.

"Hi, you look tired. Everything okay?"

He said, "I'm fine. I've been up with Allison for the past couple of days. She's been crying a lot at night; she misses mom. She's also starting to ask a lot of questions about dad. What am I supposed to tell her? I'm only a kid myself. Who was I fooling? I'm not a responsible guardian." He sighed and scratched the back of his neck. Kristin was just about to reach out and give him a friendly hug when Steve interjected.

Steve quipped, "Maybe you should try telling the truth for a change. I know you're not too familiar with the whole honesty thing, so I'll enlighten you. You see, truth is a fact or belief that—"

Josh put his hand up to silence Steve. Josh angrily said, "Why don't you shut the..."

Kristin put her hand over his mouth to silence him. She looked him dead in the eyes and give him a look. Even without any words, she could tell Josh knew exactly what she was saying. Kristin didn't want any more conflict between Steve and Josh. Sure, Steve's comment about the truth was a cheap shot, but what would yelling at him solve?

Absolutely nothing. She raised her eyebrow at Josh, silently asking him, "Do you promise you'll let it go?"

Josh glared at Steve and then looked back at Kristin.

He nodded.

She removed her hand. Kristin said, "Josh, the best and only thing you can do is a good, older brother and be there for her."

Josh nodded. "I was thinking that after school today I could get Eliza to talk. I promise that this time *I'll* get the scoop, and *I'll* record it." He looked at Steve when he said that.

"Thank you," Kristin said.

Steve said to Kristin, "We better get going. Our next class starts pretty soon."

"Yeah. Bye, Josh," Kristin said before leaving him alone in the middle of the hallway.

Chapter 20
Detective Josh To the Rescue

It was 3:30 p.m. School had ended half an hour before. Most people were outside talking on the lawn or had already left. While Josh was working on Eliza, Kristin was cornering Elizabeth. If she could just get Elizabeth to believe her, she could possibly beat Eliza for good. Elizabeth was not being receptive of anything Kristin was saying. She stood facing Kristin, arms crossed. Her dirty blonde hair was straightened.

"Elizabeth, listen to me," Kristin pleaded.

"No, you listen to *me* for once. I do not want to talk to you. Now, if you'll excuse me." When Elizabeth tried to push her way past Kristin, Kristin stopped her. Kristin begged with Elizabeth over and over. She figured she would have to give in eventually. Elizabeth would not even look Kristin in the eye. Instead, she looked everywhere else. At the ground, at her fingernails, at the ceiling.

"Lizzie, hear me out. I would never, ever hurt you. I promise. Josh, Steve, and I are trying to find enough evidence to prove it. Eliza is a mean person. Just come with me after school. Josh will have the evidence by then. If he doesn't, I'll leave you alone for good. Then, you can go be friends with that egotistical, big-headed, annoying, prestigious, fake—"

"Get to the point," Elizabeth stated. After Kristin apologized for talking meanly about Elizabeth's new "friend," Elizabeth agreed to their terms. If Josh was able to find evidence, Elizabeth would believe Kristin and help her defeat Eliza. If Josh was unsuccessful, well, they both knew what would happen then.

"I promise I won't let you down," Kristin said.

As Josh eavesdropped, he heard something interesting. Apparently, Eliza was planning a meeting at her house to "take down" Kristin on Thursday night at 7:00 p.m. Josh immediately pulled out his phone and began recording the conversation. While he was hiding (and not to mention recording), he heard Eliza tell her friends that she thought Kristin was on to her. Josh smirked. Finally, he had something on Eliza. Somewhere in his head, he was hoping that Kristin would view him as a hero if he was able to save her from expulsion. As the conversation between Eliza and her little divas went on, Josh heard Eliza say that "no one can find out about what I did, especially Elizabeth." Josh shook his head. Eliza really had turned evil, he was sure of it now. A part of him wished that maybe Kristin and Eliza could reconcile. He remembered how great they had been as friends but something told him that a friendship was the last thing Kristin would be interested in when her suspicions about Kristin were confirmed. Before he knew it, Eliza was done talking to her friends. He quickly stopped recording and put his phone into his pocket. Eliza turned the corner sharply. Josh was surprised that he hadn't heard her heels before she came. He was shocked when he saw her. Eliza eyed him suspiciously but did not utter a word. She kept walking. Josh sighed in relief. Josh was walking down the hall, on his way to tell Kristin the news. He heard faint whispering in front of the janitor's closet. He stopped. Josh looked around the hallway. No one was there. Perfect. He put his ear to the door. The person inside the closet was a male; Josh could tell by their deep voice.

"No, listen, babe... I promise that I'm just using her. The girl I love is you. I just couldn't go to the party alone. Kristin's not even my age. She's a sophomore," the person said.

It didn't take Josh long to recognize the voice. Steve. Could it be true? Steve was just using Kristin? Josh continued to listen to Steve's conversation. He concluded that Steve must be on the phone with a girl. Steve said, "Babe, I love you so much. She's not even that pretty. Kristin is pathetic. She's friendless, her ex-boyfriend cheated on her... I can go on. And, on top of that her dad died... I actually feel sorry for her. Kathy, I promise that I will dump her right after the Halloween party." Steve paused, before continuing, "No, no one can hear me. I'm in a closet. Talk to you later, sweetie. Love you."

Josh stood outside the closet. When Steve

emerged, he nearly jumped out of his own skin.

"Josh, what are you doing here?" he asked. He was trying to keep his cool.

"Who's Kathy?" Josh questioned.

"What are you talking about?" Steve asked. He had always learned to never give yourself away; it could be a false alarm.

"Don't play dumb. I know you're cheating on Kristin."

Steve replied, "Kristin and I aren't even in a relationship. I'm not cheating on her. I don't know what you're talking about. And, as much as you hate to admit it, she'd never believe you anyway. You are the guy who broke her heart, not me."

"Why are you even helping her?"

Steve said, "I feel bad for her."

Just then, Kristin approached them. Elizabeth was also with her, though she looked a tad doubtful. Steve smiled when he saw her. He was 99% sure that Josh would keep quiet, but a part of him thought that possibly Josh would out his cheating secret. "Hey, guys. Steve, I don't think you've been formerly introduced to my best friend, Elizabeth," Kristin said.

Elizabeth cringed at the world "best friend." She and Kristin were far from it but, if Kristin wanted to pretend, she could. "Steve is my... friend," Kristin concluded. "And you know my ex-boyfriend Josh. Josh and I are friends now, but I'm sure you can figure that out on your own. Anyway, let's just go to my house. I've had enough awkward conversations today to last a lifetime." Kristin began walking towards the main exit of the school. "Come on guys, don't be slow-pokes!"

Chapter 21
We Need More

Kristin stood in her room pacing. Elizabeth was sitting on Kristin's bed. Josh and Steve were both sitting on the bean bags in her room. Kristin said, "Josh? Can you reveal the huge evidence that you have? I'm dying to know. Play the recording, already!"

Josh reached into his pocket and pulled out his phone. He looked up at everyone before pressing play on his phone's recorder.

Kristin listened intently as she heard Eliza's faint voice. "Can you turn that up?" she demanded quietly.

Josh followed her instructions. Everyone in the room learned about Eliza's meeting plans to "take down" Kristin. When the audio recording was done, Kristin just stood there quietly.

Josh looked scared half to death. Would Kristin say that the recording was inadequate? Would it be enough? "So...what did you think? Am I getting promoted as a secret agent or what?" he asked.

Kristin's face stayed tight. Finally, she cracked a small smile. Josh took it as a good sign. "I'm proud of you, J," Kristin said.

Elizabeth stood up quickly, almost falling. Six inch heels rested on her feet. Kristin couldn't help but chuckle. "What are you laughing at?" Elizabeth asked in a sassy tone.

"You? You can totally not walk in heels. You almost fell! Stick to your Chuck Taylors, they're cute on you." Kristin covered her mouth to refrain from laughing even more. Finally, she let it all go. She stood there laughing for a good thirty seconds. Soon, Josh was laughing too. And then, Steve joined in on the laughing party. The only person who wasn't laughing was Elizabeth.

Elizabeth said, "Stop it! Stop laughing at me. These heels are cute. This is not funny! As Elizabeth finished her words, she cracked a smile. She began laughing along with everyone else.

"I c-c-can't breathe. My stomach hurts from s-s-so much laughing," Josh exclaimed. Everyone calmed down from their laughing fits. An awkward silence washed over the four of them.

"Thank God that's over," Elizabeth said, "I can leave now. Sorry, Kristin, Josh's audio recording proved nothing. Thanks for wasting my time. I could have been doing something useful."

Kristin quickly ran after Elizabeth. They were standing by the doorway of Kristin's room. Kristin was not about to let Elizabeth walk out. She thought they had just had a "moment." They were laughing, talking... it seemed like things were getting back to normal.

What kind of hold did Eliza have on Elizabeth

other than the first five letters of her name? "Wait, Elizabeth!" Kristin said. She paused. Looking into Elizabeth's eyes, she saw hurt.

"What?" Elizabeth snapped. She tried to not let Kristin see how emotional she had gotten. She quickly wiped her eyes.

"What's wrong? Were just laughing, and now it looks like you're about to cry And what do you mean about the recording? It proves everything. Tell me what's really wrong. I know that right now you hate me but this is a best-friend to best-friend conversation. No secrets. Just you and me," Kristin told her. She guided Elizabeth outside of her room and closed the door. She didn't need Josh and Steve listening to their girl talk. Elizabeth's face became clouded with tears. What's wrong, Lizzie?" Kristin asked. Elizabeth sniffled in response. "Whatever it is, you can tell me. Spill."

Elizabeth said, "I'm so angry at you."

"About the recording?"

"Not just that, everything! And by the way, Eliza never actually admitted to throwing the ball at me in the recording. If you're trying to win me back as a friend, I'll need to hear those exact words. Until I do, you're dead to me."

Kristin said, "Fine! When I prove you wrong, you're going to owe me a big apology."

"I'm leaving now. I hope you do prove me wrong. I'd like to think that my best friend was not shallow enough to stoop to such low levels. Good-bye, Kristin. Don't worry about walking me to the door–I know my way out."

Chapter 22
My Last Chance

Kristin, Steve, and Josh had come up with a plan to sneak into Eliza's house during her "secret meeting" with her minions. At six-thirty p.m. on Thursday, Steve would sneak into Eliza's house and distract her. Steve and Josh would then sneak up to her room and try to record her meeting with her friends. It was five o' clock now. Kristin was getting dressed in her closet. She wanted to look like a cute detective. She slid on her black Lululemon leggings, black riding boots, and a fitted black shirt. She grabbed her black Ray Bans from her dresser. Kristin then searched through her closet. She needed something else to complete the look. She spotted an all-black trench coat in the corner of her closet.

Kristin looked at herself in the mirror quickly. She made a pretty good detective. Her doorbell rang.

It was Josh. "I have something to tell you," he said as he shut her door. Kristin was a little taken aback. Josh looked genuinely worried.

"Okay. What is it?" Kristin asked.

"Steve is dating another girl. Her name is Kathy," Josh said.

Kristin burst out into laughter. After a couple minutes, she realized he wasn't joking.

"Wait!" she said, "You're serious, aren't you?"

Josh nodded his head.

"No offense, but that is an absurd accusation. Why would you even say that?" Josh tried explaining things to Kristin, but she was not buying it. In her eyes, Josh was just jealous. He wanted Kristin all to himself, and would go to extreme lengths to get her. Kristin felt herself getting worked up. Kristin said, "I do not believe you. How could you try to break up me and Steve? You know how much I like him."

"But—"

"No buts. Either you admit that you made this whole thing up, or you get out of my house. I cannot believe you. Just when I thought we were finally becoming friends."

Josh replied, "Fine! I guess I'm leaving, and I guess you're picking him."

"Leave! Steve was right; you and I can never be friends, not when you act like this. Get out! I never want to see you again."

Josh had left Kristin's house in a fury, leaving Kristin standing at her front door. Alone. She was waiting for Steve to arrive at her house. A part of her was disappointed that Josh had tried to make up something like that. She knew that he wanted to be her boyfriend, but that was definitely the wrong way to go about it. She cared about Steve a lot. He was handsome, funny, caring... mature.

Kristin finally understood why some girls dated older guys. Boys her age were immature and only interested in playing games. Kristin didn't want to play games, she wanted a real love. She had not felt a real love since Josh, and she was definitely ready to move on. Steve should have been at her house any minute. They would need to arrive at Eliza's house promptly at 7:00 p.m., so that he could distract her.

After what seemed like three years, Steve finally came. He could tell that Kristin looked a little down, but she tried to cover it up. She didn't even want to tell him about the crazy accusations Josh had made up. Kristin had read somewhere in a magazine that older guys hated drama in relationships, which is why they usually only liked girls their age. Sophomores could be so petty. Before they left her house, Kristin handed him a walkie-talkie; they would communicate through it during the "mission."

Kristin was riding in the back of Steve's car on the floor. They had both agreed that when they arrived at Eliza's car, it would be important that Eliza did not see Kristin in the car with him. The drive over had been pretty much silent. Steve seemed different. Kristin couldn't quite put her finger on it.

"Maybe he's just nervous," Kristin thought. That was the only explanation she could come up with. She felt her stomach toss and turn as the car hit tons of bumps. Steve would tell her to "get ready" whenever a bump was coming. Who knew that riding on the floor of a car could be so awful? One thing Kristin knew for sure was that she never

wanted to be in that predicament again. She wished desperately that she had someone to talk to. Josh would have been there if she had not kicked him out. Kristin was hoping Steve would not notice Josh's absence. So far, he hadn't.

Kristin realized that if she did not get the evidence today, everything would fall through. This really was her last chance. Her only chance. At some point during the car ride, she also realized that her main goal was to win Elizabeth back. She never understood how valuable Elizabeth was as a friend until she lost her. It was stupid of Kristin to be so consumed in wanting to take down Eliza. Karma would catch up with Eliza on its own. Why should Kristin stoop to Eliza's level? It was pointless. She would never be Eliza. She never could be, no matter how popular of a guy she dated. Kristin then wanted independence. She wanted to make a statement in life, even though she knew it sounded cheesy. She no longer wanted to live in someone's shadow.

"Kristin?" Steve said. The car stopped. Steve turned around and leaned down towards Kristin. Kristin looked up. Her legs felt numb from being in the same place for too long. "We're here. Stay here in the car for five minutes. After that, sneak in the house."

Maybe Kristin had not thought the plan through completely. That was one of her faults: acting impassively without thinking things through. She asked, "How am I going to get into the house?"

"It's simple. I'll make sure the door is left open, and the coast is clear. I'll try and talk to you through the walky-talkie to make sure you're in."

"Okay." With that, Steve was gone. Kristin pulled out her phone to set her phone's timer for five minutes. She suddenly felt nervous. What if Eliza figured out their plan? What if everything went horribly? The five minutes went by extremely slowly. More slowly than that one time Kristin had to have dinner with her mother's ex-boyfriend, Ricky. Kristin was dozing off to sleep when her phone's timer went off. She stiffly and slowly rose up, checking her surroundings. Quickly, she grabbed her phone and her walky-talkie. Kristin quickly sprinted across Eliza's front lawn to the front door. Sure enough, it was wide open. Kristin poked her head through the door. No one was in sight. She began walking through Eliza's main hallway. Being back into the house that she used to have sleepovers and hour long girl talk conversations in made her feel weird. Everything looked exactly the same. There were still beautiful flowers sitting in a pot on a table in the foyer. The house still smelled like a mix of vanilla and strawberries. As she stood in the middle of the main hallway, she was able to see Eliza's family room. There was still a white, baby grand piano in the middle of it. Candles lined the inside of the room's lining. The only thing that changed was that an even bigger flat-screen TV had been added to the room. As Kristin reminisced, she heard faint talking.

"Steve, why are you in my house? My friends are on their way, and they should be here any minute. Get out!" Eliza said quietly.

"Why are you whispering?" Steve asked.

Eliza said, "Cause my mom is upstairs sleeping. She's been at work all day, and she's tired. Her work schedule is draining. I would think you would have remembered that from when we were dating." Kristin felt like their voices were getting closer. Eliza's shoes were approaching. They sounded like they were coming from the kitchen. Kristin quietly bolted in the other direction. She ran into Eliza's bathroom. She closed the door and locked it. Hiding behind the door, she put her ear to it. She could hear Eliza sniffing.

"Why does it smell like Chanel perfume in my house? I don't wear Chanel," Eliza proclaimed.

Kristin heard Steve say, "Maybe your mom wears it?" Kristin could picture Eliza's face when he suggested such a thing.

"No one in my family wears Chanel. Were you at Kristin's house? She loves that perfume."

Kristin smiled. She couldn't believe that Eliza actually remembered.

"Anyway, I came by because I wanted to chat. I've been thinking... and I'd like it if we could talk about... us," Steve said.

Kristin was sure that this was only his way of distracting Eliza. Steve and Kristin had talked about her relationship with Josh, but had not gone into detail about Steve and Eliza's.

Eliza replied, "You do? Why do I feel like you're lying?" Steve was able to distract Eliza with conversation for awhile. He was also able to get her out of her house and onto her patio. Kristin ran up Eliza's stairs. Oddly enough, she felt at home. It'd only been a few months since she'd been in Eliza's house, but those few months felt like years. Kristin knew her time was running out; Steve could only stall Eliza for so long. She was running into Eliza's bedroom when she heard Eliza talking.

"I'm serious Steve, get out of my house. This whole thing has been a waste of time. I have a meeting with my friends." Eliza shouted.

Steve replied, "W-w-wait." Kristin could hear Eliza coming up her stairs swiftly. Crap! Kristin began having a mini panic attack. She heard Steve following Eliza up the stairs. "Eliza, I didn't finish. I really don't think it's a good idea that you go upstairs."

Eliza paused on the stairs. "And why not? God, I always knew you were a tad strange, but ever since you started hanging out with Kristin, you've become ten times weirder." Eliza continued walking up the stairs.

Kristin ran into Eliza's huge walk in closet. It was probably the size of the average person's master bedroom. Kristin hid behind a clothes hamper. She pulled a ton of clothes, which were hanging on hangers, down from above her and piled them around and on top of her so that she was not easily seen. As she pulled down a pair of jeans, she noticed the tag still on them. She nearly squealed. Eliza had the new pair of dark wash Dona Clide jeans. Dona Clide was only the best designer in the entire world. The pair of jeans that Eliza had weren't even available in the US yet. They were only being sold in Europe at the steep price $300. Premium denim wasn't cheap. Knowing Eliza, she'd had one of her mother's assistants fly to Europe and buy her a pair. Typical Eliza. Contrary to Eliza, Eliza's mother was extremely kind. Well, unlike the "new" Eliza. The old Eliza could be bratty at times, but had an extremely warm heart.

Kristin snapped out of her thoughts. She heard a set of footsteps near. They must have been Eliza's. Then, another set of feet followed, probably Steve's.

"Steve, can you leave? Why are you in my room? Get out of here!" Eliza shouted. "I'm calling the cops, I swear."

Steve asked, "Where are the pictures of me?"

"What?"

"I heard your walls were still covered with my face. Guess it was a rumor?" he asked.

She said, "Guess so. Do you smell that? It smells like Chanel perfume in here! I swear if I'm being burglarized by some poor, 15 year old girl–"

Steve interrupted, "Why would a poor girl be wearing Chanel?" Eliza scoffed.

"Stop diverting the subject."

"But, you brought it up," Steve pointed out. Eliza began rummaging through her desk drawer. While she was doing that, Steve pulled out his phone. He needed to contact Kristin. Where was she? He was awful at stalling. He sent her a text message, and within seconds Kristin's ringtone began playing from Kristin's phone. Kristin pulled the phone out of her pocket and tried to silence it, hoping Eliza had not heard. She opened the message and quickly replied.

Steve - Where r u? time is running out!!

Kristin - In her closet! Help!

Eliza said, "Did you hear that? It sounded like Selena Gomez. Ya know, one time I met her when I was visiting my grandparents in Texas. She's so nice."

"Um, yeah." Steve awkwardly scratched the back of his neck. Eliza made her way over to her closet. "Where are you going?" he nervously asked.

"To my closet? I have to look presentable for my friends. Look, if you insist on staying here for whatever reason, at least don't be annoying," she said. Eliza entered her closet. Kristin stiffened. Eliza began wandering in the sweaters section of her closet, which was directly across from where Kristin was hiding. Eliza began tapping her finger on her chin, trying to decide on what to grab. She walked away from the sweater section and over to where Kristin was. Eliza gasped when she noticed all the clothes that were in a huge pile.

"My cleaning lady seriously needs to do her job," she muttered. Eliza rolled her eyes. She began reaching over Kristin, searching through the clothes that were hanging over her. "Where are my Dona Clides?"she whined. Kristin was hoping that she would not notice the jeans were on top of Kristin's head. Kristin crossed her fingers and hoped for the best. Couldn't Steve help her? He knew she was in the closet.

Moments later, Steve walked into the closet. "Eliza, there's something important I need to tell you," he said. Truthfully, he didn't even know what he was going to say.

"What is it?" Eliza asked.

"I can't tell you in here. I.. have a thing with, um... closets. I'm highly claustrophobic," Steve rambled.

Kristin found herself on the verge of bursting out into a laughing fit. Listening to Steve try to convince Eliza to leave her own closet was pure enjoyment.

Eliza muttered, "Fine! Make it quick."

Kristin did not realize she had been holding her breath the entire time until Eliza left the closet. She gasped for air quietly. While Steve talked to Eliza about God knows what, Kristin figured that it'd probably be best that she stayed in Eliza's closet during her "secret meeting" with her followers. After all, there was no other place in Eliza's house that she could eavesdrop on Eliza's conversation and record it sufficiently. Now, the real problem would be escaping. Kristin was not quite ready to think of that yet. Her first challenge had not even been accomplished yet.

After Steve had left Eliza's house, Kristin realized she was in her situation alone. If she failed, no one would suffer the consequences except her. Her fate was up to her. As scary as the whole situation seemed, Kristin had faith in herself. She was still sitting in the same exact spot as before. Eliza had walked into her closet twice and chosen an outfit. About fifteen minutes later, Eliza's friends arrived–Meg, Sara, Lillianna, and Portia. Kristin immediately recognized their voices, especially Portia. Who could forget such an annoying, squeaky voice? Kristin knew exactly why Elizabeth was not invited. She couldn't be in attendance of a secret meeting that was primarily about herself.

"Hello, ladies," Eliza said to the four girls as they sat on the lavish couches in Eliza's room. Kristin turned on her phone's audio recording. "I have snacks downstairs, but food is not a major concern as of now. We'll eat later. Besides, some of you could use some starvation. I have a secret to tell you guys."

"Oh! A secret? Like what? Are you getting engaged? Do you have a secret boyfriend?" Meg wondered. "I wanna be a bridesmaid. Oh my god, this is gonna be so much fun!" she shouted.

"Why are you so stupid? You think I'd have a meeting to announce me getting a boyfriend? Please, Meg. I'm starting to wonder why I even like you in the first place. Remind me," Eliza said.

Kristin rolled her eyes as she listened. Who on Earth would tolerate someone treating them like this? When Kristin and Eliza were friends, they treated each other as equals.

Meg said, "Because I have that beach house in Maui that you like to use on the weekends."

"Oh, yeah. I forgot. Anyway, I don't have a boyfriend. Portia already knows my secret, but I think it's time I share it with the rest of you. I did something that you guys are going to think is despicable but, I did it for a good cause. You guys know how there's that trial tomorrow? For, Kristin?" All the girls nodded their heads. Eliza continued, "Well, I have something to admit. I know that Kristin didn't throw the ball."

Kristin silently screamed in joy. Finally! She finally had what she needed. The four girls, except Portia, gasped louder than they would during the sale in Saks.

Lillianna asked, "How do you know that?"

It was the question that Kristin knew the answer to. The only way Eliza could possibly know that Kristin didn't throw the ball would be if... "

"I threw it myself," she simply said. A silent hush fell upon everyone. Even Kristin was shocked to actually hear the words. It was surreal. A moment for the books, for sure.

Chapter 23
This Is The Day

Kristin stared at herself in the school bathroom. There were only ten minutes left until the trial began. The feelings that she felt were a mix of things. She felt confident, yet worried; excited, yet afraid. She was all jumbled up. She kept imagining how great it would feel when she was finally proved that she had been telling the truth. As she found herself pacing back and forth, she thought of her father. She missed him so much. He was her rock, her everything. Losing him at such a young age had thrown off Kristin's whole childhood. And as she stood in her designer wear, she then realized that in a heartbeat she'd trade all the fancy clothes, cars, and the mansion, if she could have her father back. Kristin wanted to make her father proud, even though he could not be there to cheer her on. She wanted to win the trial and show him that she could do anything. She'd been smart enough to sneak out of Eliza's house without being caught; she would hopefully be smart enough to prove her guilty. As Kristin was quietly rehearsing what she would say, she heard footsteps approaching. She looked up and found Elizabeth walking into the bathroom.

"Lizzie," Kristin started, "I have something to tell you. I was telling the truth about the dodgeball thing. I have proof!"

Elizabeth put her hand in the air to signal her to stop talking. "Kristin, please. I'll believe it when I see it."

Kristin said, "Believe me, you will."

Kristin stood backstage in the school's auditorium. The trial was starting in a matter of seconds. Surprisingly, butterflies weren't erupting in Kristin's stomach. She felt nervous, but not too much. She stole a quick glance at Eliza, who was standing backstage on the opposite side of the auditorium. Almost all her friends were surrounding her. In the midst of all that chaos, Eliza still managed to keep herself together. Kristin could hear the loudness coming from the auditorium. The entire school was sitting in there, waiting to vote on Kristin's destiny. Her mind began to wander all over the place. Where was Josh? Was he still mad at her? Even if he wasn't, she was still mad at him. Who did he think he was? Kristin knew that he still had feelings for her, but accusing Steve of cheating was low, even for Josh. Kristin than began to think about the fact that even if he had "cheated" on her, it barely qualified as cheating, since they were not even dating. Even so, she'd still be extremely hurt if it was true. Steve was charming, handsome, sweet... in a way, he reminded her a lot of what Josh used to be like when they were dating. She knew it was foolish of her, but she was starting to really like him. Everything about him was perfect. Almost too perfect. Soon enough, it was time for her to enter the stage. As she walked carefully in her five-inch heels, she looked out into the audience. The stage of the auditorium was set up like a jury room, except for the fact that the "jury" was not on the stage. Kristin sat down in her place, while Eliza sat about twenty feet away from her. Principal Edwards introduced the case to the entire school.

"By now, most of you probably know what happened to one of our best students, Elizabeth Showers. Elizabeth was in her gym class, when she was–for lack of a better term, knocked out. We all know that this school puts a huge emphasis on safety, so what happened to Elizabeth is unacceptable. There's been a lot of rumors about who threw the dodgeball. My hope is that this trial will put all the rumors to rest and find out who really did it. The two girls who are sitting on the stage seem to have the answer. They'll be making cases against to each other. Shall either one of them interject while the other is speaking, I will intervene. At the end of this all, you will get to vote. Whoever is found guilty will be immediately expelled from the school," he said.

Kristin's entire body tensed up. All of a sudden the nerves were coming back. Despite that, she felt slightly confident. Josh had emailed her the voice recording of the evidence he had of Eliza. Plus, she had Eliza's voice admitting she'd thrown the ball. There was no doubt in her mind that Eliza would be completely caught off guard. And, of course Elizabeth would forgive her in a heartbeat.

Everything would happen perfectly. She and Steve would go to the annual Halloween party together, eventually start dating, eventually become a couple, and eventually get married. Kristin knew she was going a little overboard with the marriage part, but there was no harm in dreaming, right?

"We will begin with the plaintiff–Eliza McKinley," Principal Edwards said.

Kristin felt herself shrink.

When Eliza stood get up and the entire auditorium erupted with cheer. Why was everyone always on Eliza's side? Surely they would not be on her side after Kristin made her speech. Eliza stood up and walked to the middle of the stage. Her minions, including Elizabeth, quickly came from backstage carrying a huge poster board, which was covered by a large cloth, and a stand to set it on. After they had arranged the poster on the stand, they walked off stage. Eliza held in her hand a huge pointer. Kristin hadn't even thought to use props; she just barely could come up with a speech.

Eliza slowly pulled the cloth off the poster board. She stood in the center of the stage. Kristin's jaw dropped when she realized that the poster was covered with a gigantic blow-up picture of her own face. What made her cringe even more was the fact that the photo was taken from Kristin's ninth grade yearbook. Ouch. The morning that the picture was taken, Kristin woke up with two, enormous pimples on her face. It wasn't the most beautiful snapshot of Kristin, to say the least. When the picture was unveiled by Eliza's perfectly manicured hand, the entire audience giggled uncontrollably. Kristin swallowed, trying not to look embarrassed. The old

Kristen would have been worried about what the picture would do to her reputation. The old Kristin was self-centered and materialistic.

"Is that picture really necessary?"Principal Edwards asked.

Eliza nodded quickly. She used her pointer to draw more attention to the photo.

"This," Eliza said, "is Kristin Gregory. Most of you can barely recognize her. She's changed so much recently. However, ninth grade Kristin was a simple girl. Her best friend at the time was Elizabeth Showers and surprisingly enough, me as well. I'm sure you're all wondering why I was ever friends with her. Well, I'll tell you. Kristin was my best friend until I found cooler people to hang out with. Eventually, those cooler people graduated. Now, I'm the most popular girl in school. Kristin has been trying to take me down ever since. That's why she is framing me. Kristin wants me to become just as lame as she is," Eliza stated. She paced back and forth. She was so confident. How did she do it? Kristin had no idea. Public speaking had never come naturally to Kristin. Eliza continued, "On the morning of Elizabeth's sad, sad injury, Kristin had a very intense argument with Elizabeth. Elizabeth's sweet sixteen was approaching, and instead of being a good best friend, Kristin decided she'd skip Elizabeth's party. Obviously, this sparked some tension between the girls. Kristin knew she was going to potentially lose her best friend. Kristin and Elizabeth had been friends for years. They've laughed, even cried together." Kristin took a deep breath as Eliza continued. Eliza had barely started and it seemed to be better than Kristin's argument. Eliza picked back up with her talking. She explained that Kristin and Elizabeth had had a nasty fight.

Principal Edwards said, "I have to ask you something, Eliza. I understand that Eliza and Kristin were in a fight, but why would that lead her to do something so drastic?"

Eliza replied, "I'll tell you. You see, Kristin was secretly torn between Lianna's sweet sixteen and Elizabeth's sweet sixteen. So, she thought it would be smarter to get rid of Elizabeth temporarily, so she wouldn't have to choose." Kristin nearly exploded when Eliza said this. It was possibly the craziest thing she had heard. The crowd, however, seemed to be enjoying everything that came out of Eliza's cunning mouth. Later, when Eliza referred to Kristin as a "pure mean girl", the audience erupted in laughter.

A young girl added, "She's the meanest girl in the school." Kristin felt ashamed of how she had acted. Honestly, she was a mean girl. She cared about the wrong things. Having everyone hate her really changed that. She wanted more than anything to be able to go into the past and change her actions. Going through her fight with Elizabeth made her realize that life is too short not to be nice to others and value those you love. Everything else was just noise. Kristin felt her hands get clammy as she listened to Eliza continue. She had to admit that Eliza's argument was strong. She'd been able to use all sorts of props and diagrams. Kristin watched as everyone listened to Eliza intently and soon felt small.

Kristin looked out into the audience for Steve.

Oddly enough, he was missing. Where was he? Earlier, he'd promised he would be in the audience to cheer her on for moral support. The one person she did spot was Josh. Why did it seem like he was always there for her? Steve was the one who she was going to the Halloween party with, not Josh. Kristin heard the audience erupt in applause. Eliza had made her case, and it had taken all of fifteen minutes. Kristin's heart began to beat fast. It was her turn. Finally. Her vision seemed to black out for awhile. Kristin felt like the world stopped for a couple of seconds, that's how nervous she was. She made her way over to the podium. It was time for her to prove her innocence. Although she was nervous, she was confident that the audio recording she had managed to get would surely convince everyone.

"Hi, I'm Kristin. First off, I'd just like to apologize to everyone I've ever offended, hurt, or been rude to in the past year," she said, "I, um, I've been caught up in everything. I'm genuinely sorry. I know that my apology cannot make anything better, but it's a start. Mostly, I'd like to apologize to my best friend, Elizabeth. Lizzie, the way I treated you is unbelievable. I should have never considered going to Lianna's party in the first place." Kristin saw the tiniest of smiles spread across Elizabeth's face. Kristin went on to further explain the argument between the girls. She was sure that she'd done a better job of doing this than Eliza, since Kristin was actually the one in the fight. "Yes, I was mad at Elizabeth. I was extremely mad. We both were. That's normal for friends when they fight." Kristin turned to Eliza and said, "Eliza, when we were friends, we fought, didn't we? We could stay mad at each other for days. What I am trying to say is that fights are normal. I mean, haven't any of you ever gotten into a fight with your friends? True best friends always get past them, just like how Lizzie and I were going to eventually get past our fight. No matter how mad I was at Elizabeth, I would have never tried to hurt her. I know none of you will believe me, but I have proof. I managed to get Eliza admit to throwing the ball."

Eliza blurted, "That's impossible. I didn't do it."

Principal Edwards quickly made her sit down so that Kristin could play the audio tape. Kristin pulled out her phone and pressed, play. She put her phone to the mic, so that the entire auditorium could hear. Eliza's voice was a little muffled on the recording, since Kristin had recorded the entire thing from a closet. Eliza's voice filled the entire room via the recording.

The entire audience gasped when they heard Eliza's voice say, "Because I threw it myself." Kristin stopped the recording.

She said, "I hope that proves everything. You all may not like me, but you know that it would be wrong to not punish Eliza." She spotted Elizabeth in the audience, who now had tears flowing from her eyes. Eliza soon was on the stage hyperventilating. She scurried off the stage quickly.

Chapter 24
Victory

Kristin won the case, needless to say. She walked out of the auditorium, to be immediately greeted with a huge hug from Elizabeth. Elizabeth was still crying. Kristin was so happy to have her best friend back. The girls embraced. Kristin was also relieved to know that Eliza was leaving the school. Permanently. For the past year, she had been burdened with the way she had lost her friendship with Eliza. She now knew that all the drama was over.

"Kristin?" Elizabeth cried, "I'm so, so sorry. I b-b-believed Eliza over you a-and–"

Kristin stopped her midsentence and replied, "It's okay. We were both wrong. I'm sorry too. I love you, Lizzie. You're my best friend." Moments later, the girls were laughing and joking like nothing had ever happened. They were both happy to have all the fighting in the past. They were filling each other in on what was going on in their lives, when Eliza walked over to them. They stopped conversing immediately. Kristin sent Elizabeth a

238

"what does she want" look, and Elizabeth shrugged her shoulders. Kristin had never seen Eliza look so distraught, besides the time when her pet goldfish, Gucci, died. Her makeup was smeared, due to crying.

Eliza said, "I'm sorry, Elizabeth."

"Don't apologize to me. I believed you. I knew I was stupid for doing that. I never want to see you again," Elizabeth spat.

Kristin folded her arms.

"Elizabeth, even though we were only friends again for awhile, it reminded me of old times. I missed you. And Kristin, I missed you too. I'm sorry for all this. I'm going to be out of your life forever."

Kristin quietly asked, "Why did you do it?"

"I was jealous of you. When I first stopped talking to you guys, it was because I thought it was for the best. I was mean to guys for no reason. And I've always regretted it. And, when I realized that you two only grew closer without me in the picture, I was even more jealous. You guys went on without me. It was like I never existed. I guess I did all this to get back at you, Kristin. And now, I'm kicked out of school. This is the worst thing that has ever happened to me."

"Thank you for the apology. I forgive you. I'm trying to move on in life. All this petty drama is stupid. And, of course I missed you. You were like a sister. I spent so much time trying to take your spot in the school, and it just wasn't worth it. I'm sorry that you have to leave school, but you hurt a lot of people—especially Elizabeth and I." Kristin stated.

"I understand. I'm sorry... again."

"Me too." Eliza wondered, "Do you think we

Ashleigh M. Garrison

could be friends again?"

"I don't really know at this point, Eliza," Kristin said, "We're in different places right now."

Eliza nodded. "Well, I've got to go pack my things. I guess this is good-bye–forever." Eliza began to walk away, when she suddenly turned. "Actually, I take back what I said a couple of seconds ago about my expulsion being the worst thing that has ever happened to me. Losing your friendship is by far the worst thing that's ever happened to me. Bye, guys."

Kristin and Elizabeth waved at Eliza. Kristin smiled, realizing a small chapter in her life was ending. The "Eliza chapter" was finished.

Chapter 25
You were Right

Later that night, Kristin was ready for the Halloween party. She had asked Elizabeth to join her, but Elizabeth had other obligations with her parents for the evening. The girls had planned to get together the next day. Kristin had decided that her costume would be that of a Hollywood actress. It was basically an excuse for her to dress up and wear pretty clothing. Her hair was in huge curls, and she had on light makeup. She was wearing a pink dress that had glitter lightly dusted on it. She had paired it with white pumps and simple gold jewelry to complete the look. It looked like the night was going to be a good one. Steve and Kristin were going to dance, have fun, and enjoy themselves. Kristin would talk with all his friends, she hoped. The party started at eight, and it was currently seven forty five. As Kristin finalized her look, she thought of Josh. Surely, he would be at the party. One thing was certain: it was going to be extremely awkward seeing the guy who tried to tear apart she and Steve. Kristin walked into her mother's room.

"Mom," she asked, "Do I look okay?"

Her mother looked up from the book she was reading and smiled. Her glasses were resting on her nose, while her long hair was pulled back into a cute bun. Kristin smiled at the sight of her mother relaxing. Her work schedule had been so ruthless. "You look beautiful. I think you need a necklace. Here, let me go see what I have in my jewelry box." Her mother went over to her massive jewelry collection. She pulled out a pendant-shaped diamond necklace. Kristin nearly squealed at the sight. The pendant had been in her family for generations. It was only passed down to the girls in the family when they got married. Wearing it before marriage was extremely rare.

"I can't wear that, Mom. You know it's a tradition."

"I don't care. You look beautiful tonight, and this necklace will make you look even better." She placed the piece of jewelry on her daughter's neck carefully. "Have fun tonight, baby. Give Steve a hello for me."

Kristin stepped out of her parked car. Steve's house looked amazing with all the Halloween decorations on it. Steve was right, he had somehow managed to pull the whole thing off. His entire property was filled with teenagers. Most of them went to their school but there were a lot of people she didn't recognize. She could hear the music blasting loudly. A few people even said hey to her as she walked up the pathway to his house. Maybe people were finally beginning to start liking her again. Kristin skimmed the crowd for Steve. Where was he? This was supposed to be their date. A couple of football players greeted her. Josh definitely was not there. She had heard from a few people that he had skipped the party. Phew. She was relieved. After what seemed like a half hour of looking for Steve, she decided to grab something to snack on and then go search for him.

Kristin roamed the inside of Steve's house. Something told her to check in the kitchen. As she neared it, Kristin thought she heard his voice. She called out, "Steve? You in here?" When he didn't reply, she continued walking towards the kitchen.

She heard him mumble into the phone, "I love you too, Kathy. Talk to you later, babe." Kristin stopped dead in her tracks. Steve looked up, a look of guilt on his face.

"I cannot believe you. Josh was right. I'm out of here," she snapped.

"Wait!" he called.

He rushed over to her and put his arm on her shoulder. "Let me explain, babe."

"Do not touch me, you jerk. And, I have no clue who that Kathy girl is, but I feel bad for her. Guys like you disgust me!"

Kristin sat in her car crying. Why? Why did Steve turn out to be a jerk? The bad thing was that she'd once had strong feelings for Steve. Maybe she should have listened to her gut instinct and left him alone. The whole night was a waste. She felt empty. Just when she started to begin to fall for him, he broke her heart. Turns out everything did not work out the way it did in movies. Kristin started her car up and drove to the only house she could think of.

As she stood on the doorstep of the house, Kristin wiped her eyes. After ringing the doorbell, she paced back and forth. The door quickly swung open.

"Kristin?" Josh blurted. He was wearing baggy shorts and a muscle tee. He took Kristin's presence in. "You look stunning. What happened? Why do you look so upset?" Kristin simply wrapped her arms around him and starting crying. After a couple of seconds, he hugged her back and tried to comfort her. Even though he didn't know what was wrong, he knew that it was only right for him to be there for her.

Kristin and Josh sat comfortably on his couch. She had a cup of hot chocolate in her hand. Both of them were underneath blankets. Josh had listened to her when she vented and explained her heartbreak.

"Josh, I know you tried to warn me. I was stubborn. I guess I was caught up in the thought of him. You were trying to protect me. You poured my heart out to me; you told me you still loved me. I was awful to you," she explained.

Josh said, "It's okay. Oh, and I think it's time for me to fess up about the whole cheating thing." Kristin looked up at him. "Eliza threatened me. My mom and her dad were working out a business deal–a very important one for my mom. I knew it would be awful if it fell through. She probably would have wanted to be near me less than she already did. Eliza wanted to hurt you, so she made me kiss that girl in the gym. She said that if I didn't, she'd make sure my mom's career ended. I know it was stupid of me to fall victim to Eliza and her threats, but I caved. I love my mom. I couldn't be the reason that she didn't get that deal."

"Josh, I cannot believe you did that for your mom. That's great. Why didn't you tell me?"

"I was embarrassed. I know you don't love me back, but I'll always love you."

Kristin grabbed his face gently and pressed his lips to hers. The fireworks were still there, only stronger this time. He quickly kissed back and she wrapped her arms around his neck. After a little while, they both pulled away.

"I love you too," Kristin said.

THE END

Ashleigh M. Garrison, who credits her parents for motivating her to read, has had a passion for writing since elementary school when she began writing short stories. Her love for the craft grew over the years. She came up with the story line for *Dodgeball Mystery* while in the fourth grade and finally breathed life into it.

Ashleigh, a sophomore at International Academy, lives in Detroit, Michigan with her parents. She is currently working on her next project.

CPSIA information can be obtained
at www.ICGtesting.com
Printed in the USA
FFOW03n1005150716
25824FF